SWEET
SOMETHINGS

Connie Shelton

Books by Connie Shelton

THE CHARLIE PARKER SERIES
Deadly Gamble
Vacations Can Be Murder
Partnerships Can Be Murder
Small Towns Can Be Murder
Memories Can Be Murder
Honeymoons Can Be Murder
Reunions Can Be Murder
Competition Can Be Murder
Balloons Can Be Murder
Obsessions Can Be Murder
Gossip Can Be Murder
Stardom Can Be Murder
Phantoms Can Be Murder
Buried Secrets Can Be Murder
Legends Can Be Murder

Holidays Can Be Murder - a Christmas novella

THE SAMANTHA SWEET SERIES
Sweet Masterpiece
Sweet's Sweets
Sweet Holidays
Sweet Hearts
Bitter Sweet
Sweets Galore
Sweets Begorra
Sweet Payback
Sweet Somethings
Sweets Forgotten
The Woodcarver's Secret

SWEET
SOMETHINGS

The Ninth Samantha Sweet Mystery

Connie Shelton

Secret Staircase Books

Sweet Somethings
Published by Secret Staircase Books, an imprint of
Columbine Publishing Group
PO Box 416, Angel Fire, NM 87710

Printed and bound in the United States of America
ISBN 1500512303
ISBN-13 978-1500512309

Book layout and design by Secret Staircase Books
Cover illustration © Marishaz
Cover cupcake design © Makeitdoubleplz

First trade paperback edition: July, 2014
First e-book edition: July, 2014

As always, my undying gratitude goes to those who have helped make my books and both of my series a reality: Dan Shelton, my partner in all adventures who is always there for me, working to keep the place running efficiently while I am locked away at my keyboard. My fantastic editing team—Susan Slater, Shirley Shaw, and proofreader Kim Clark—each of you has suggested things that help me see something new in my writing. Stephanie and Ashley—I love our brainstorming sessions—we will do great things together.

And especially to you, my readers—I cherish our connection through these stories.
Thank you, everyone!

Chapter 1

This festival will be the death of me yet, thought Samantha Sweet as she wrung the neck of a pastry bag full of chocolate icing. When she'd first heard of Taos's Sweet Somethings chocolate festival she envisioned a lovely park-like atmosphere, with colorful booths displaying masses of delectable chocolates, maybe Willie Wonka music setting the tone—something no one from three counties would be able to resist. What she'd gotten was last-minute responsibility for a committee that was operating weeks behind schedule.

An acquaintance of Sam's had recommended that she become involved and Sarah Williams, the poor lady who'd let everything fall behind, had leaped at the suggestion with all the gusto a four-foot tall-woman with a bad hip could manage. Sarah was a dear older lady and they had become friends during the past few weeks—she was just not much of an organizer. When she practically begged Sam to take over, it hadn't been the lure of the festival that persuaded

Sam to do it; the real reason was something else entirely, Sarah's connection to an old woman Sam had met only once and a carved wooden box with mystical powers. Sam had been trying for a long time to learn more.

Now, with each tinkle of the front door bells in her bakery showroom, Sam could hear the volume of voices increase as her committee members arrived. Six p.m. but her day was far from finished. She cleared the last of her tools from the worktable and picked up the thick folder of notes from her desk. The folder flopped open and Sam scrambled to retrieve a half-dozen small scraps of paper that drifted to the floor, the tidbits that held the event together at this point. She shoved the notes back into the folder and fought back a wave of panic.

How did I let myself get talked into this, especially on such short notice? She pushed through the curtain separating the kitchen from the showroom and willed the corners of her mouth upward.

"Sam! Thank you. Can we get the meeting underway now?" Carinda Carter pushed forward through the group and met Sam with a challenge in her stare. It was the way Carinda approached everything, Sam had discovered—long on assertiveness and short on tact. 'Thank you' coming from Carinda implied 'thank you for finally showing up.'

"Is everyone here?" Sam scanned the faces in the room. In addition to herself, Carinda and Sarah, the committee consisted of Harvey Byron who owned a boutique ice cream shop on the Taos Plaza and two of Sam's trusted friends, Rupert Penrick and Erica Davis-Jones. Riki, as she was known, owned the dog grooming business next door. Sam's daughter, Kelly, worked for Riki and often pitched in with the committee work as well. Sam spotted Riki and

Kelly through the front windows so she called the meeting to order.

"Okay—reports," she said. "Rupert?"

"The venue is set—*finally* got the signed contract for the Bella Vista Hotel. I tell you, girl, it was a challenge to get the manager to sit down for two seconds." He handed a few pages to Sam.

She knew she would get an earful of details later but, truthfully, she didn't care. The original plan to hold the chocolate festival at Kit Carson Park had fallen through, then the weather forecast called for temperatures in the nineties and it turned out the convention center was already booked. She'd pulled in every contact she could think of to find a place with the right ambiance and location. The Bella Vista Hotel was actually outside of town—located in a bucolic spot with the Rio Fernando running beside it—but at least it had a ballroom large enough to accommodate most of the vendors. The park-like setting could provide additional places for outdoor booths where non-meltable products might go. Now to entice the crowds to this somewhat out-of-the-way place.

Carinda Carter was twitching in her seat at one of Sam's bistro tables and had her hand in the air.

"Yes, Carinda? Can you fill us in on how the designs are coming along?"

The rail-thin woman stood up, sent Rupert a long look—as if the delay in securing the venue were all his fault—gave a toss of her chin-length auburn hair, and picked up a poster-sized sheet of paper. She held it up for all to admire.

"The logo, as you can see, places whimsical hearts and swirls against a rich background of purple. I've shaded the lettering to represent all varieties of chocolate, from a creamy white to a deep brown. Details—here you see Sweet Somethings in large type." She ran a finger across the face of the poster, like one of those super models who point out the prizes on TV game shows. "The dates—nice and large, just here. All I was waiting on was the name of the venue—" Another glare toward Rupert. "I will fill that in and get it to the printer in Santa Fe as soon as I can. Of course the tickets, the programs, banners and vendor ID badges will all follow the same theme. I only hope that our printer hasn't booked so much other work that he can't get to ours now that we're running so late."

Carinda faced Rupert again and opened her mouth, but the large man was not known for taking guff from anyone. He met her challenge with a steely gaze.

Sam swallowed a retort. "I'm sure there are many printers. We'll find someone." She cleared her throat and turned to Kelly. "How about the radio ads?"

Kelly consulted a list. "We've booked five days of spots with KVSN during their 'Taste of Taos' show and their 'Visions' program. Since the festival benefits charity, I got them to double the number of ads at no additional cost. We'll be running these the two days leading up to the festival and the three days during. And we've got Riki lined up to do interviews with stations in Santa Fe and Albuquerque."

Although Riki wasn't directly involved as a vendor or participant, the British transplant had such a charming accent that people always listened. She would be excellent as the voice of the festival.

"Good job." Sam preened a little on her daughter's behalf. "Rupert, I believe you have something else for us?"

Never one to shy away from the limelight, the six-foot man in the purple tunic and soft beret stood up and sent another glare toward Carinda.

"I do have some exciting news. Early this morning I received the letter of agreement—and, I might add, a check—from *Qualitätsschokolade*, the famed Swiss chocolate manufacturer, as the official sponsor of our festival, and the provider of prize money!"

A murmur went through the group.

"With what they sent we will be able to award two thousand dollars …"

A ripple of wows.

"… for third place. Three thousand for second place. And a stunning five thousand dollars for first place!"

A collective gasp. Kelly, Riki and Carinda were scribbling notes.

"Additionally, I pulled in a favor from the editor of the summer tour guide to do a cover spread and feature story on the winner of the People's Choice award."

Carinda almost came out of her seat. "We never talked about—"

Sam held up a hand. "It was an idea Rupert came up with after our last meeting. Letting the crowds vote on a favorite item—it encourages their participation. The magazine story—wow—an excellent prize."

Carinda gave a semi-gracious smile and leaned back in her chair.

Rupert wasn't finished. "I have also contacted the bestselling novelist Victoria DeVane, who has graciously consented to provide medals of gold, silver and bronze to go along with the prize money. *And* she says we may hold a raffle, with the prize winner's name to be used in Victoria's next book." He sent a smug look toward Carinda. "*That* should bring in some extra money."

Sam covered her own smile by looking down at her folder of notes. She was the only one who knew that Rupert himself was the famed writer. It didn't matter; the important thing was that finally it looked as if the festival really would come together and it would be a prestigious one at that.

Harvey Byron spoke up. "Will the prizes be limited to candy or pastries?"

"Any item containing *Qualitätsschokolade* products will qualify."

Harvey's wheels seemed to be turning. Sam imagined that his popular brownie nugget dark chocolate supreme ice cream would soon—if it didn't already—contain chunks of the Swiss maker's own delectable cacao bars. An award, especially if it came with a magazine write-up, might be the thing to launch Harv's dream of expanding his ice cream shops statewide and eventually nationwide. The tall, slender man had confided this in his reticent manner once when Sam had stopped by Ice Cream Social for a cone. He was a nice guy, she'd decided, with soft brown eyes and sandy hair; she just didn't see the hard-driving personality that would propel his business to the national level.

Rupert hadn't sat down yet. "Carinda, you'll need to add the prize information to the poster. Oh, and change that background to royal blue, the sponsor's color."

Carinda sputtered and put on her martyr face, making it clear that she felt saddled with the burden of last-minute changes. No one but Sam seemed to notice.

Kelly spoke up. "Should we put out a call for entries, try to get more vendors?"

Sam looked toward Rupert.

"Ooh. Limited basis, okay? We're already pushing our limits since the Bella Vista venue is a lot smaller than the places we originally considered."

"I'll do one quick advance press release."

Carinda faced Kelly. "Can you handle that? I mean, *I* really have the experience."

"I'll be fine." Kelly's voice came through clenched teeth.

Sam looked back at Rupert again. "So, our vendor signups are coming in?"

"Better than expected. Of course you'll be there, right? Sweet's Sweets is the best bakery for a hundred miles."

Sam had been working on a few new recipes, herself. "Becky and Julio have been baking up a storm. We will definitely have a booth." Another aspect of this whole thing that she'd never done before—setting up displays and sales staff outside of her own bakery. "But I won't enter the competition for the prizes. It doesn't seem right since I chair the committee."

Did she only imagine a satisfied smirk on Carinda's face? For someone new in town, the little whippet had certainly inserted herself quickly where she hadn't been invited.

The discussion turned to decorations, where Sarah Williams had agreed to take charge by forming her own little subcommittee of older ladies who enjoyed making garlands and flower arrangements and such. That group would also arrange for people to serve as ticket-takers at the gate when the show opened.

When the conversation trailed off into specifics about what colors the flowers should be, Sam tapped her pen on the table top.

"I'm sure everyone is eager to get home but there's one more item for tonight." She thought of her husband; recently, poor Beau had prepared his own dinner more nights than she wanted to admit.

"Judges. Especially now that there is prize money on the line, this will be important."

She turned to Harvey, the committee member she had assigned to the task last week, but Carinda piped up first.

"I'll be happy to judge," she said. "I was told by the chocolatier at Le Patisserie in Paris that I have an excellent palate."

"Thank you, Carinda, but if we can find outsiders I think that will give the necessary impartiality."

The woman sank back in her seat, her mouth once more forming a straight line. Sam turned to Harvey again.

"Well, I'm still working on it," he said, a nervous tic working at the corner of his mouth. "So far, I've asked two people but I don't have commitments yet."

"Can you call me when you know for sure, Harv?" She looked up at the group as a whole. "It's only a week, folks, and we have a lot to do. Feel free to call me with updates, and let's plan to meet again on Thursday."

Chairs scraped and feet shuffled. Sarah Williams edged past Kelly and Riki and touched Sam's arm.

"I'm so sorry I flaked out. This has put a lot of work on your shoulders."

It had, but Sam didn't see much point in acknowledging the fact.

"Mary Raintree told me that you were hoping to talk with me about Bertha Martinez and I'm so sorry we haven't found a minute to do that yet," Sarah said. "I apprenticed under Bertha, you know, before I went to college and became a nurse. She was a wonderful healer and even in my practice of Western medicine I frequently used her techniques. Many of my older patients preferred the old ways."

A wistful look came over her face. "I've often wondered about an old box she had. She kept herbs in it. Bertha told me the box had made a great journey."

Sam felt a rush of excitement—*this* was the subject she'd really wanted to discuss. She had briefly met Mary Raintree a few weeks ago in her quest to learn more about the powers of a wooden box that had been given to her by a local woman believed to be a witch. Mary, herself a practitioner of Wicca, had pretty well convinced Sam that Bertha Martinez was actually a *curandera* in the old Hispanic tradition. Now she was beginning to understand why Mary thought it would be a good idea for her to speak with Sarah.

"I can see that you know of it," Sarah said.

Sam glanced sideways; the other committee members were too near.

"We will talk about it later." Sarah patted Sam's arm then turned to leave.

"Yes, I definitely want to." Sam watched the older woman walk out the door. Finally—she would get the answers she had been seeking.

Chapter 2

Sam drove home, her thoughts leaping every direction. With the hundreds of unfinished tasks for the chocolate festival and Sarah's enticing statement about having known Bertha Martinez so well, her mind wouldn't settle on one thing. She picked up a pen and tried to jot a note when the name of another possible contest judge came to mind, but the flash of oncoming headlights warned her that writing and driving do not mix. She tossed the pen onto the passenger seat and concentrated on watching for the turnoff to the ranch home she shared with Sheriff Beau Cardwell, her spouse of eight months.

"Hey, darlin'," he greeted her at the front door, "you look whupped."

Their border collie and Lab rushed out to nuzzle her hands, seeking out the sugary essence that followed her everywhere after a day at the bakery. Beau pulled her into his arms and stroked her back as she melted into his chest.

"I'm so sick of working with this committee," she mumbled into his soft plaid shirt. "I thought a couple of them would come to blows awhile ago."

"Come inside. I'll get you something to eat while you shower."

She couldn't remember the last time she'd eaten anything more substantial than a muffin—probably breakfast, fourteen hours ago. No wonder she looked and felt like a limp rag. So, why was it that she could never seem to shed these extra twenty pounds?

Beau handed her a wine glass. "Relax, sweetheart."

She dropped her backpack purse onto the sofa in their big log-walled greatroom and headed upstairs, sipping the cabernet.

Ten minutes later she descended to find a TV tray set up in front of her favorite chair, a sandwich and bowl of soup waiting.

"It's nothing fancy," he said, holding up the wine bottle with an offer of a refill.

"It's fantastic just to sit down and eat," she said. "I used to stand in front of the fridge and snack on cheese and pickles before I met you."

He settled in the corner of the sofa nearest her. "So . . . festival planning getting you down?"

"We're just so far behind. And then there's this one woman who wants to micro-manage everyone else. She's criticized Kelly's choice of radio ads, Harvey's choice of contest judges, and started to give Rupert a little flack. He withered her with one of his famous stares."

"How'd you get stuck with her anyway? She somebody

important in town?"

"No—that's the thing. Nobody knows her. She just showed up. I get the impression she just moved here, she's traveled a lot—or gives that impression—and wants us Taos locals to be in awe of her sophistication." She took a huge bite of her turkey sandwich.

"Maybe she's just lonely—new in town and all that. She wants to pitch in and get involved."

"Yeah, probably. Just pure luck that I'm the one she gets to drive crazy."

"Hey, it can't be as bad as dealing with the Flower People. We got word that they've chosen Taos County as the rendezvous point for their summer love-in or whatever they call it."

Sam pictured the number of aging hippies who had settled in the area after the '60s, most of them now with grey hair and crusty, sandal-clad feet. They shopped at the health food store and plastered their cars with bumper stickers protesting everything but were generally good citizens.

"I assume you aren't talking about the locals," she said between sips of her soup.

"I should be so lucky. What I hear, this bunch numbers in the thousands and they show up to camp out and salute the sun or pray toward the moon, or some such thing."

"That sounds harmless enough."

"Probably is, except they don't exactly respect fences or bring their own bathroom facilities or park their vans in designated areas. In Idaho, where they camped one year, the town spent thousands of dollars cleaning up after them—trash by the truckloads, human waste in open pits and trampled crops didn't exactly endear them to anyone nearby."

"Can't you just chase them out?"

"Me and four deputies? If they choose public land I can probably get some help from the Forest Service. Problem is, those agencies usually issue them a permit when they're told it will be a 'family reunion' of twenty people. By the time they figure out how many have really arrived, they're overwhelmed too. And, of course, all it takes is one landowner to give them permission to use private property. The ranchers love the offer of money—we hear that the group usually puts up a deposit of a thousand dollars or so with a promise to pay more when they arrive—then the guy figures out what a mess will be left behind, and the little bit he collects doesn't begin to cover the cleanup."

Sam wiped her mouth with a napkin and stood to carry her dishes to the kitchen. Suddenly, Carinda Carter didn't seem like such a bad deal.

Beau took over kitchen duty, suggesting that Sam go on to bed. Upstairs on the master bath vanity sat the carved wooden box Sarah Williams had mentioned as belonging to the old *curandera*. Sam thought back to the day it had come into her possession, the day she had unsuspectingly broken into Bertha Martinez's supposedly abandoned house to find the old woman there, dying. She'd hesitantly accepted the odd, ugly box as a gift from the old woman and brought it home.

The first time she opened its lid and ran her fingers across the interior edges an electric-like shock zapped through her body. That night was still a blur, but the strange artifact had changed her life forever.

Now, her thoughts turned again to Sarah Williams and the older woman's comment about the box. Should she admit to Sarah that the old *curandera* had given it to her? She snuggled under the quilt and fell asleep contemplating the question.

* * *

When her alarm went off at four-thirty, Sam suppressed a groan, sorely tempted to roll over and let Julio handle the bakery. The baker she'd hired last fall, despite his arms full of tattoos and the deafeningly loud Harley he roared up on each morning, had a key to Sweet's Sweets and could certainly handle the pre-dawn duties. He'd quickly mastered all of her standard pastry recipes and could turn out enough muffins, scones, coffee cake and croissants to satisfy the breakfast crowd, giving Sam the chance to sleep in until Beau awoke. Never an early riser, Sam appreciated the extra couple of hours.

However, these last four weeks had become so full of festival duties that the only hours of the day in which Sam managed to decorate cakes and test new recipes were those early mornings before her phone began to ring incessantly. Today, she wanted to work on a batch of chocolates with a Taos motif—flavored with chile and shaped like miniatures of the famed Taos Pueblo, she hoped they would appeal to locals and visitors alike. The challenge had been to tweak the recipe so that the bitter-dark chocolate wouldn't melt in the early June heat. Each time she thought of it, she wanted to snarl at the Chamber of Commerce genius who'd chosen the date for the event. Clearly, the person was no chocolatier.

She splashed cold water on her face and finger-combed her short, graying hair, grabbed an apple from the bowl on the kitchen table and patted each of the dogs on the head before starting her van and heading for town.

In the alley behind her shop she found Julio's motorcycle in its usual spot and the scent of cinnamon and sugar wafting out the back door. He greeted her with his usual quiet "morning" and went on inserting trays of blueberry and cranberry scones into the bake oven. Sam slipped into her baker's jacket and grabbed ingredients from the shelf above the stove, along with her favorite saucepan.

Within a few minutes the cacao, sugar and butter were bubbling softly. Sam kept one eye on the candy thermometer as she reached for a small tin box on the upper shelf. In it she had stashed three small cloth pouches—secret ingredients given to her a year ago by the quirky Romanian chocolatier who had shown up one Christmas and vanished just as mysteriously. She had no idea what the mysterious translucent powders contained, only that they made her chocolates irresistible to the palate. When Julio walked to the showroom with a tray of apple muffins, she quickly took a pinch from each pouch and stirred it into the mixture on the stove. A moment later the chocolate was ready for tempering, that all-important process of rebinding the fats in the cocoa butter, the reason good chocolate is resistant to the whitish bloom that can mar its appearance. She poured the molten mixture onto the cold surface of her tempering stone on the worktable just as the back door opened and her daughter's face appeared.

"Hi, Mom. Just thought I'd check in and see if it's okay if I smash the face of that Carinda Carter?"

"Not until after the festival, Kelly," Sam said without missing a beat. She smoothed the cooling mass of chocolate with her spatula. "What's the problem?"

"Last night I was assigned the radio spots, right? Coordinating and approving the ads?"

Sam nodded, not taking her eyes off the chocolate.

"So, this morning I call the station and find out that Carinda was there yesterday. She's changed everything I did! And she never mentioned this at the meeting, at all."

"Did you change it back? Or did she have some valid ideas?"

"Well, some of her stuff wasn't so bad . . . it's just so . . . so frustrating and embarrassing to have her override me like that."

Sam judged that the chocolate was ready to rest. She turned toward Kelly.

"I know. Carinda comes across as a little sharp in her manner."

Kelly's mouth opened.

"But—maybe she just wants to fit in here in town. I gather that she hasn't been here long and she's probably just wanting to join in, to help."

Kelly gave a little growl. "Maybe."

"If the ads don't contain any actual errors, we could let them ride. There's enough new work to be done that it's a waste of time to go back and re-do other tasks, right?"

"Okay, okay. But I'm keeping an eye on that woman."

Becky Harper, Sam's chief decorator, arrived just as Kelly stomped out the back door with an expression that didn't exactly indicate the Carinda matter was closed.

"What was that about?" Becky asked as she hung her purse on one of the wall hooks and slipped into her white baker's jacket with the Sweet's Sweets logo embroidered on it in purple.

"More chocolate festival dramatics," Sam said. "Why is it that doing anything by committee is such a pain in the neck?"

She handed Becky a stack of pages, the bakery's normal orders for the next couple of days, then reached for her candy molds. While she gently poured the newly tempered chocolate into small pueblo-shaped molds, Becky organized the written order sheets.

"Looks like we have two weddings this weekend and a birthday cake for a guy whose hobby is competitive shooting," Becky said, spreading the pages on the worktable.

"Julio has already baked the layers for one of the weddings—the square ones. He'll bake the other cake once the stock breakfast items are done. You'll need two dozen sugar daisies and a bunch of full-blown pink roses for the first one. The other requires a lot of string piping—you want to give it a try?"

Becky sent her an uncertain look. "Strings? They're so tricky."

"It's okay. I can do those if you'll just pre-make all the flowers and get them into the fridge to set up."

Becky sent her a grateful smile and arranged the order sheets in the sequence they would be completed. "For the competitive shooter, his wife brought those photographs that Jen copied and attached to the back. The lady didn't really have any idea what she wanted, but Jen and I talked about it. I think I could make the shapes of the metal targets they use in his competitions. They're just outlines of simple animal shapes—a chicken, a pig, a turkey and a ram. We could make them out of chocolate and put them up on a stand on top of the cake. Unless you think some type of a bulls eye target is better? And, of course, his name and all that."

"I like your idea of the silhouette targets," Sam said,

carrying her tray of molds to a cooling rack to set up.

Down in her pocket her phone rang before she had turned around.

"Sam, hi, it's Carinda Carter."

Goody. Sam felt her smile go a little frosty.

"Just wanted to report that I made all of *Rupert's* changes and I've sent the art files off to the printer in Albuquerque. They'll have our finished posters, the tickets, the badges—the whole works—done by the end of the week."

"That's great, Carinda, but weren't you going to send them to me first? Just to double check everything?"

"I didn't see much need for that. These guys have a great reputation and said they could get right on the job if they had the materials this morning."

Sam took a deep breath. "Okay, then." *It's not as if I need the extra tasks on my own list.*

"I just need to know where to have the invoices sent."

As far as Sam remembered, they had not yet discussed the budget for the printing; this question should have been asked way before Carinda took it upon herself to give the job to a printer. She took another deep breath. They were so far behind schedule that details such as costs would have to work themselves out. She gave Carinda the name and address of the Chamber's treasurer.

Stuffing her phone back into her pocket, she had to agree that Kelly had a valid point about Carinda's pushy ways. A shriek from the kitchen grabbed her attention. A large tub of buttercream icing lay splattered all over the floor and Becky stood with a look of shock on her face.

"It slipped right out of my hands," she said with a moan.

"Let's get it cleaned up. Just be careful where you step—

the stuff is slippery as all get-out."

Before they'd finished mopping the floor with degreaser, Sam's phone rang three more times. *Why* had she asked the committee members to report their questions and problems?

Lunch time came and went; she'd been half-hoping to hear from Beau and escape the kitchen for an hour or so, but he was probably running a dozen directions as well. Last night he'd sounded none too happy about the potential invasion by the Flower People. She hoped his day was going all right.

By four o'clock she and Becky had finished the two wedding cakes, which were now safely stored in the fridge until their delivery times; the sportsman's cake was looking like a cute little miniature target range under Becky's capable hands; and Sam found a moment to check the sales room where a glance at the register totals showed that her assistant Jen had been busily ringing up sales all day. She'd heard from nearly every one of the Sweet Somethings committee members and dispensed advice the best she could. The only one of them who had not contacted her was Sarah—the one she most wanted to speak with after their abbreviated conversation the night before.

She found a moment to step into the shade in the back alley, where she pulled out her phone and dialed the older woman's number. It rang several times and she was mentally composing the words to leave a message when a strange male voice answered.

"Who is this?" Sam asked. "I may have gotten the wrong number."

"Were you calling Sarah Williams?"

"Yes, is she home?"

"I'm her nephew. Marc Williams. I'm afraid I have bad news."

Sam's gut did a twist.

"She's in the hospital," Marc said. "She collapsed at home this morning and called my father. I came rushing over and called the ambulance. I came back by her house now for her insurance information and such."

"I just spoke with her last evening and she seemed fine," Sam said. "What do the doctors say? Will she be okay?"

"At this point they're still running tests. Her heart seems strong and she says she's always been really healthy, except for that flu last winter. But I have to let you know—she's not doing too well right now."

Sarah had never mentioned a nephew; maybe she would feel more secure if a friend were also at her side.

"Could I go by and see her?"

"Um, sure. I suppose that would be okay."

She told Marc Williams she would get there right away. A dozen images flashed through Sam's mind after she hung up—the conversation last night, the wooden box, old Bertha Martinez. Months of looking for answers about the box and its origins, and Sarah seemed like her first firm lead. If something happened to Sarah now, Sam would never get those answers.

Chapter 3

Sam got into her van and pulled to the end of the alley behind the bakery, debating. The hospital was to the south, but if she took an extra fifteen minutes she could dash home first and get the box. She turned left and made her way along back roads until she came to the turnoff for her driveway.

From the bathroom vanity she retrieved the box and held it between her hands until she felt warmth begin to suffuse her skin. The normally dull wood took on a golden glow, the usual sign that it was sending its healing power to her. She dumped out her bits of costume jewelry and carried the box to the kitchen where she retrieved one of her canvas shopping bags and set it inside.

At the hospital she followed the directions Marc Williams had given her, down a corridor to room 278 on the left. In bed, Sarah looked even smaller than normal. The lump under the blanket was more than two feet from the end of the bed, and her stocky body had melded into the mattress. Even her round face seemed slack, her mouth in an unaccustomed downturn and her eyes closed. A man in his forties stood over the bed, speaking earnestly to Sarah.

"You must be Samantha," he said when he spotted her in the doorway. "I'm Marc."

Sam shook his hand but glanced nervously at the inert form. "How's she doing?"

Sarah stirred and mumbled something. Giving it another try, she cleared her throat. "I . . . fine."

"Hey, Sarah. It's Samantha."

The older woman's mouth tried to form a smile. Watching the effort, Sam felt her heart tug.

"The doctors say she had a stroke," Marc said. "It's good that she's speaking a bit now, but they have more tests to run."

"I won't stay long," Sam assured him.

"Go 'way, who you are." Sarah didn't lift her head but the meaning in her slurred words was clear enough. "Tha man. Who?"

"Aunt Sarah, it's me, your nephew. Just take it easy."

"It's fine," Sam told him. "Grab some coffee or something. I'll stay until you get back."

"Darn thing, Sam," Sarah muttered. "Ba timing."

"I brought something," Sam said, setting the canvas bag on the floor near the bed. She reached for Sarah's hands with her own and squeezed them. One squeezed back, the other remained limp. As she ran her hands along Sarah's arms, she felt her own warmth travel to the other woman.

Sarah's right fingers twitched a little.

Sam pulled the carved box from the bag and set it on Sarah's abdomen, then placed each of her hands on top of it. The box showed no reaction. She picked it up and held it close to her own body and the golden glow returned to the wood.

Sarah gasped and turned her head toward Sam. "It's Bertha's! The box did the same thing when she handled it." This time her speech was perfectly clear.

"I don't know how long the effects of it will last, Sarah. Can you tell me more about it?" Sam set the box beside Sarah and used the bed's controls to raise her head a bit. Already, the older woman's eyes seemed sharper, her face more alert.

"Bertha told me she'd had this box since she was a young child. A favorite uncle sent it." She paused, thinking. "She studied the *curandera* ways from her grandmother. *Abuela*, she always called the old woman." Her eyes took on a faraway look and Sam felt a pang of impatience.

"She was a wonderful teacher . . . I learned so many things that modern nursing school didn't teach."

"Why didn't she leave the box with you? I only happened to show up at her house on the day she died. She insisted that I take it."

Sarah had not taken her eyes off the box.

"It needed the right person. Bertha told me that. I handled it many times but it never did the same things for me."

"I wonder how she knew it would be me?" Sam didn't realize she'd said the words aloud until Sarah responded.

"She believed in the power of the mind, even though

hers slipped in her final years. She probably wished that the right person would come to her. You did."

As part of a contract Sam had with the Department of Agriculture to clean and maintain abandoned houses, she had been assigned to the home of Bertha Martinez. No one realized the old woman, barely alive at that point, still occupied the place. When she discovered the dying woman Sam had been nearly frightened out of her wits. But in retrospect, Bertha had seemed to expect her arrival. After insisting that Sam take the box, she had passed on within minutes. Had the power of her mind engineered those events?

"I was traveling at the time," Sarah said with a glance toward the door. "When I got back Bertha was gone, her house empty."

"I'm so sorry. We tried to locate friends and relatives but couldn't find anyone."

"She became reclusive. Kids would tease her. People were sometimes afraid of her."

Sam nodded, remembering what she had heard at the time about the rumors of Bertha being a witch.

Sarah gave another quick look toward the open door, then lowered her voice. "There were two boxes, you know. My father saw one . . . many years earlier . . . during the war."

"I want to know about that one, too," Sam said eagerly.

She'd come across one in Ireland last fall—could it be the same? She wanted to ask more questions, but noticed that Sarah's eyes were closed once more.

"You should rest," Sam said. "I'll come back when you're feeling better."

She ran her hands across Sarah's shoulders and along

her arms and the older woman settled down with a relaxed look on her face. She'd just set the box back into her canvas tote bag when she looked up and saw the nephew standing at the doorway. How much had he observed?

"I just spoke to the doctor," he said. "They'll be taking Aunt Sarah downstairs for some type of a scan fairly soon. What did she say to you?"

Sam brushed aside the question, gave him her phone number and asked him to stay in touch, especially if anything about Sarah's condition changed.

She drove away from the hospital pondering the improbability that Bertha had somehow willed her to walk into the house at exactly the right moment to receive the magical box. Evidently Sarah, the one person who had been aware of its power, was fine with the idea that Sam had become its keeper.

She was halfway back to Sweet's Sweets, wondering when Taos had developed such a crush of rush-hour traffic, when her phone rang. Her first thought was of Sarah but the readout showed Rupert's number.

"I may have just located a celebrity judge for the festival," he said immediately. "What would you think about Bentley Day—huh?"

Sam's mind went blank.

"Star of that California-based reality show, *Killer Chef*?"

"Is that about killing or about chefs?"

"You've never seen it? Samantha, dear, what planet are you living on?"

The one that doesn't have the TV on every second of the day. "Sorry," she said. "Guess I'm not exactly up to date. How did you manage this?"

"Okay, so Bentley isn't really Australian. He's just got a really good handle on the accent. He grew up in Santa Fe and his mother is a dear friend from the art gallery crowd. I gave the brat a ride once, all the way to L.A. He was in college, mind you, but mama didn't want him on a plane right after nine-eleven. So, now I'm calling in the favor."

"And people in Taos will know who this guy is?"

"People across the *continent* already know who this guy is, honey. He'll be a big draw for ticket sales."

The whole reason the Chamber of Commerce had dreamed up this event in the first place was to donate the ticket proceeds to a children's cancer charity. No one could argue with any possible means to sell more tickets.

"That sounds excellent, Rupert. Thanks."

"I need two more, Sam . . ."

"Sorry, it can't be me. I'm chair of the committee, and I'm there as a vendor. You've got to go for unbiased candidates. Check with Harvey and see if he's found anyone else."

"Well, I'm determined to find a couple more that will so *far* outshine our argumentative Carinda that including her won't even be an option."

"I sincerely wish you well." She clicked off the call and pulled in behind the bakery.

Jen was in the process of closing out the register; Becky had left a note about an unfinished cake, promising she would come early in the morning to get it done; Julio was stacking clean baking pans in readiness for the morning routine. He said goodnight and a moment later she heard his Harley rumble away.

"You look tired," Jen said when Sam walked into the showroom. "I don't know how you're keeping up with all this."

Truthfully, Sam didn't quite know either. In times past, she'd occasionally called upon the powers of the wooden box to energize her to get through holidays and other job stresses. Recently she hadn't touched it, until today. Apparently, all of its energy had passed along to Sarah in the hospital just now.

Jen handed Sam a zippered bag with the day's receipts before circling the room to switch out lights and flip over the Closed sign on the door. By the glow of soft night lighting they walked through the shop and out the back door.

At home she found a note from Beau with an arrow pointing to the refrigerator. Inside, a large bowl of salad, covered in plastic wrap, had another note on it. "Had to run out, don't wait on me." Cute. They texted each other so much these days that a handwritten note felt something like an old-fashioned love letter.

She set the salad bowl on the countertop and scooped half of it onto a dinner plate, added her favorite poppy seed dressing and settled on the couch in the great room. The earlier conversation with Rupert reminded her of something and she picked up the remote control and switched on the TV. She could record an episode or two of *Killer Chef* to find out what the fuss was all about.

As it turned out, according to the guide, one of the channels was running a marathon and Sam got her first look at Bentley Day the moment she clicked over to it. The diminutive man in kitchen whites and a tall chef's hat stood in the middle of a high-end kitchen full of stainless steel and oversized kettles, with piles of colorful vegetables strewn about the work surfaces. With a deep tan, possibly enhanced by makeup, and shaggy blond hair he certainly fit the part of some rugged outbacker. He boosted the image even further as soon as he opened his mouth, spewing a rant of four-letter demands at the three young cooks in white hats who stared back at him with varying degrees of animosity. Did the man not worry that all of them held large knives as he berated them?

Sam stared in fascination. Apparently the goal of the show was for each of the contestants to prepare an outrageously complicated meal, while having their chopping and dicing techniques critiqued by Bentley-the-expert. As he hovered over them, they shot evil looks toward him and toward each other.

At a commercial break halfway through, Sam set her salad aside and called Rupert.

"Seriously? This Bentley Day person is obnoxious and foul-mouthed. We can't have him at the chocolate festival. We're hopelessly small-town polite here. He'd never fit in."

"Samantha, dear, all that stuff on TV is scripted. The accent, the language . . . it's all written down and he's merely acting the part."

"Yeah, but if the point is to bring a celebrity chef here as one of our judges, won't people expect him to be the same character they see on his show?"

"We'll write him a script that leaves out the f-words, okay? With the Aussie accent and wearing his *Killer Chef* white coat, he'll still be a big hit. Besides, I've already gotten his mother to tell him that he *will* do this."

"If you say so . . ." Sam didn't even try to keep the skepticism out of her voice.

"Trust me, dear heart."

He hung up and she went back to the show. Muting the volume helped some, and the segment where a food fight began in the kitchen only moments before the dishes were to be judged actually added enough tension to keep her eyes firmly on the screen. When the next episode began, Sam turned off the set. She knew how this worked. If she watched three of them she would begin to feel for one of the contestants—probably the young girl who seemed so browbeaten by Bentley—then in another episode or two this girl would become the villain as she took up gossiping about her competition. Eventually, one would begin to emerge as the 'nice' one and—ooh, surprise—by the end of the season that person would be the winner and everyone in the land would end up happy. Really. She'd watched Kelly sucker in for way too many of these setups.

She called Rupert again as she walked into the kitchen. "In addition to striking our celebrity's colorful language, please be sure that he understands there are to be no food fights and no pretending to get sick on any of the entries. He has to behave himself, start to finish."

She put her dinner plate into the dishwasher.

Rupert started to say he would handle it but Sam found herself distracted by the sound of tires on gravel out front. A moment later the front door opened, closed sharply, and Beau's boots stomped across the room. She told Rupert goodbye and walked into the living room.

"What's up?" Sam asked when she saw Beau standing by the wide French doors that faced the back deck.

"I can't believe it!" He stared into the deepening dusk. "Old man Mulvane is letting them in—just like that!"

"Them?" Sam's mind hadn't quite left the *Killer Chef* scene.

"And he wasn't even going to tell me! I found out because Max Rodriguez called awhile ago, when I was making the salad for dinner."

"I'm afraid I'm not really putting all this together," she said, standing beside him and leaning into his field of view.

"Sorry." He took a deep breath. "Okay, you know that the property bordering us on the west is Max's. The sixty acres to the east belongs to old man—uh, Bruce—Mulvane."

She nodded, although she'd barely met either of the ranchers.

"So, Mulvane just gave permission to the Flower People to use his land this year. Last year, up near Del Norte, Colorado, over a thousand of them showed up and stayed two months; they overran several neighboring farms and did so much damage that the landowners are still trying to get restitution. That will never happen—these are the free-love, free-everything types who don't think anything should cost money. It'll be a miracle if they don't cut our fences and ruin the grazing land the horses need."

"Why on earth would Mulvane agree to this?"

Beau shook his head and paced across the room. "I was over there just now . . . I've been hearing that he's slipping a little." He tapped the side of his head. "Thought I could talk him out of it, but he had a contract."

"Really?"

"Yeah, they may be anti-establishment, but somebody in that group knows a bit about legalities."

"What can you do about it?"

"I don't know, but they'll probably start showing up this weekend."

Chapter 4

Sam had no trouble waking up Thursday morning at four-thirty. Beau had tossed and turned all night long. She spent the morning at Sweet's Sweets, going into high gear. While she cooked, tempered and molded chocolate pueblos and flavored creams, Becky and Julio worked to stock the shop for the next two days. Next week they would be baking triple batches of cakes, brownies, cookies and cheesecakes.

"If the festival doesn't bring in huge crowds, we'll have inventory to last until Christmas," Becky said as she helped Sam box up the chocolates.

"I sure hope not. I won't exactly be able to sell these as fresh beyond next week. We might have to brace ourselves for an all-time big sale."

"It'll work out. Don't worry. Everyone in town *loves* your recipes. They will turn out in droves."

Speaking of droves, Sam thought of Beau's concern over cattle getting into his alfalfa fields if the invading hippies should break down the fences. She knew he'd planned to go to the courthouse this morning to see what he could legally do to keep them out. And as long as her mind was on the subject of out-of-control situations, she remembered that her unharmonious committee was set to meet at Carinda Carter's apartment this afternoon. She let out a sigh and tried to envision a day, somewhere in the future, where all this drama would be a thing of the past.

Carinda had emailed her address to everyone—a small set of duplexes on a quiet side street not far from Sam's old house where she'd lived for nearly thirty years before marrying Beau and moving out to his ranch. Sam parked in one of the outer slots marked for visitors, noting a few other familiar vehicles. She tucked her burgeoning file folder under one arm and picked up the bakery box of sugar cookies she'd brought along in hopes of keeping everyone happy.

The eight units formed a square around a neatly landscaped patch of ground with colored lava rock for ground cover and xeriscape plantings, some of the few things that were doing well in the current drought. The back windows of each apartment faced the parking area, while the front doors were accessed by walkways at each of the four corners of the square. Sam found Carinda's place by following the sounds of loud chatter.

"We should wait until Sam arrives before we get into all this," came Riki's voice through the screen of the open front door.

"Sam is here," she announced, holding out the box of cookies.

She stepped into a tiny living room where Carinda had placed dining chairs and two plastic ones from her front porch in order to accommodate everyone. So far, in addition to their hostess, the group consisted of Riki and Kelly, Harvey Byron, and herself. Sam gave a quick version of the reason Sarah would not be attending, an unsubtle way of letting them know they would each need to absorb a few extra duties.

Rupert arrived with apologies for being late, giving the tiny apartment and its rental-grade furnishings a critical eye. Sam shot him a look and hoped Carinda didn't notice. Not everyone lived on the scale that Rupert indulged in.

"Okay, everyone, let's get started so we can all get home at a reasonable hour," Sam began. "I understand that the advertising materials have been sent to the printer?"

Carinda nodded. "I'll have them tomorrow. I can use some help to get them put up around town." Without waiting for volunteers she called upon Riki, with a withering look which hinted that the groomer had done precious little so far.

Sam spoke up. "All of us have businesses to run and our time is limited." *Except for you, Carinda.* She didn't say it. "Let's divide the posters equally and each of us can be responsible for a few. Put them up in your own shops and whatever other public places where they're allowed."

Riki sent Carinda a triumphant little look. Sam went to the next item on her agenda.

"Harvey? Anything new with the judges?"

"I'm happy to say that I've confirmed two—the police chief's sister and the mayor's wife. They both seem very excited about it, but I'm afraid I'm stumped for a third. But worst case, I know I could get my brother to do it."

He blushed deeply. "Sorry, I didn't mean that would be the worst case at all—"

"It's okay, Harvey. None of us took it that way." Sam glanced toward Rupert. "We actually have a lead on someone—something of a nationally known face—that we might be able to get. Rupert? Do we know anything more about that yet?"

"We're all set." He stood up to make the announcement, having never forgotten his roots in theatre. "We, dear committee members, will be graced by the presence of none other than Bentley Day, star of *Killer Chef*."

A couple of gasps went up, but Sam was pleased to see Harv's blank expression too. At least she wasn't the only person in town out of touch with reality TV.

Naturally, Kelly was one who reacted. "Oh my gosh, Bentley Day! I wonder if he'll bring that huge chef knife he always carries around."

Riki spoke up. "Oh, can't you just see him whacking into the cakes and pies with that thing—cutting out slices for the judges to taste?"

"Oh, man, this will be great!" Kelly said.

Riki, Rupert and Kelly, all fans of the show, began trading best episode quips. Carinda, no longer the center of attention, sat with her mouth clamped firmly shut, while Harvey and Sam seemed to be the outsiders. Sam gave them a minute and then called everyone back to attention.

"I need someone to contact Sarah's friends who were making decorations and find out how that's coming along. The deadline is next Thursday, and there should be a place where one of us can pick up everything. I can use my bakery van for that, but I won't have time to run around to a dozen different women's homes."

Kelly looked up from her notepad. "I'll do it. Somewhere in my notes I think I jotted the names of those ladies." She flipped pages and Sam mentally checked one item off her list.

"The other thing is the venue. Sometime in the next couple of days I'll get out there and look over the layout, sketch out a floor plan and figure out how the booths will be laid out. I'm hoping vendors can begin setting up Thursday afternoon, since the gates open at ten o'clock Friday morning. But I'll go over all that with the hotel manager. Does anyone else have questions or something to report that we haven't covered?"

Carinda, to no one's surprise, spoke up. "If Bentley Day backs out, my offer still stands to be a judge."

Rupert took a deep breath, ready to rebut the insinuation that he'd chosen a flaky judge, but Sam beat him to it. "Thank you, Carinda. We will certainly keep that in mind."

"In fact, maybe it would be better to have four judges anyway," the woman went on.

"Carinda, what are you thinking?" Rupert said. "Everyone knows that a judging must have an odd number, in case there are ties. Bentley Day will be the perfect person to act as tie breaker between two local, female judges. It's all settled." The way he crossed his arms over his chest, along with the fact that several others were nodding, left no room for discussion.

Carinda's expression froze somewhere between embarrassment and hatred as she stared at Rupert. Sam sent her a faltering smile before glancing around the room and adjourning the meeting.

"I'll catch you later, Mom," Kelly said under her breath. She turned to Riki, who must have been her ride over here from work.

Rupert swished one of his signature purple scarves across his left shoulder, looked down his nose at Carinda, and walked out.

Why does he have to do that? He can be such a diva sometimes.

Sam gathered her pages of notes and looked up to see that everyone had cleared out quickly. Carinda clattered dishes in the small kitchen alcove just off the living room.

"Sorry about that last bit," Sam said. "Here, why don't you keep the rest of the cookies?" The box still felt nearly as heavy as when she'd brought it, a testament to the tension among those in the room. Rupert and Kelly alone would have normally polished off more than half of them.

"No one appreciates my work, do they?" Carinda said with a catch in her voice. "I try so hard and they really don't care."

"It's not that," Sam said without much conviction in her voice. "They just don't know you."

Nor did they want to, she realized.

She heard a loud sniff and saw tears trail down beside Carinda's beak-like nose. *Oh boy.*

"I never seem to fit in, no matter where I go. It was the same way in my own family—nobody really wanted me there."

Sam restrained a long sigh. She *so* badly did not want to be this woman's therapist.

"Carinda, your designs for all the printed materials were wonderful. I'm sure you'll impress the hell out of the group when they see the finished product." She spotted a box of tissues on an end table and handed one over. "Don't let

Rupert's attitude get to you. He's not usually that way . . . probably just having a bad day."

"You think so?" Carinda blew her nose loudly. The tears seemed to be waning.

"You'll see. Planning things is always a little tense but once the festival starts, it'll be so much fun that everyone will forget these little squabbles."

"Really?"

"Really."

Sam knew this was her exit line. Otherwise, Carinda would start to see them as all chummy and might do something drastic like asking her to stay for dinner.

"So! I'll go get my husband fed, and I'll see you in a day or so, whenever you want to drop off those posters at my shop." She beat a path around the side of the building and got her van in gear as fast as she could.

Beau wasn't home when she arrived so she set about her plan for putting him back in a good mood. His favorite fried chicken, mashed potatoes and green beans—just the way his mother had always made for his birthday. Everything was nearly ready when he came in, and she gave him a glass of his favorite Scotch before putting the food on the table.

"I'm guessing by the look on your face that you didn't accomplish much at the courthouse," she said as she handed him the potatoes.

"I got a little lecture from the judge, along the lines of 'don't waste the court's time with questions you already know the answers to'."

"But you were just—"

"He was right. No law has actually been broken yet. I knew that. With that contract the Flower People have the right to go onto Mulvane's land. Until they come onto our place they aren't trespassing. Until they cause damage, they can't be cited for that either."

She reached out and squeezed his hand.

"If I were being called out to anyone else's land this is exactly what I would have told them. I jumped the gun by going to the judge, so I guess I'm grumpy because he called me on it. He did drop the hint that it would be perfectly within my jurisdiction to post a couple of uniformed officers out here, to keep an eye on things and to catch them in the act if they get out of hand." He sighed. "Like I have the manpower for that. I have one more approach to try, but it would have to involve a different judge."

Sam nibbled at her chicken.

"And then there goes my whole weekend," he said. "I had the days off, and I was planning to help you at the festival."

"Really? You would do that?"

"It was a thought." He smiled, the one that had originally made her fall in love.

"Well, play it by ear. Maybe the hippies won't cause any trouble at all."

Whether it was the fried chicken dinner or the kind words, Sam didn't know. She did know that he was in an amorous mood later and they made it an early bedtime. When she woke up before her alarm the next morning, feeling unbelievably refreshed, she decided to get an early start at the bakery.

Two wedding cakes and eight dozen molded chocolates later, Sam looked up in surprise when Jen peered through the curtain from the sales room.

"A lady's here, asking about someone on your festival committee . . . I think. I'm not really sure what she wants."

Sam didn't recognize the tall, blonde woman who stood in the front of the shop, eyeing the display of cakes in the front window. City dweller, was Sam's first impression. Designer shoes with six-inch heels, a deep red dress that fit her slim body perfectly, a haircut and color job that had to have cost a couple hundred at least. No one in Taos dressed like that.

"Hi, Ms. Sweet? I'm Kaycee Archer." She held out a hand with hundred dollar nails on it. No, definitely not from around here. "I'm sorry to interrupt your work, but I'm looking for someone that I believe is here in Taos."

And I'm the logical person to have this information?

"I was told that she's involved with an upcoming festival and that you're the person heading it up. Her name's Carinda Carter."

"I do know her."

"Wonderful! I need to contact her on another matter. I suppose you would have an address or phone number for her?"

Sam almost pulled out her phone to recite the number stored there but something held her back. For all she knew, this city slicker was selling insurance or cosmetics or something like that.

"If you'll give me your card, I'll be sure to pass it along to her when I see her again."

Kaycee didn't seem thrilled with that plan but she pulled a pen from the tiny purse hanging by a thin cord from her shoulder. She reached for a napkin near the cash register and scribbled a number on it. "Tell her the call will be financially beneficial to her."

Hmm. Insurance, it was.

Sam took the napkin and watched the woman walk

out and get into a nondescript sedan parked in front of the bookshop next door. She started to crumple the napkin but thought better of it. The decision wasn't hers to make. Carinda could easily throw the saleslady's number away herself.

"Nice shoes," Jen said. "Completely impractical. But nice." She gave that if-only-I-lived-in-a-city sigh that wasn't uncommon around here.

Sam sent her a smile. "Since I'm out of the kitchen already, I think I'll run out to the Bella Vista Hotel and go over some things with the manager. Carinda Carter may stop by with a stack of posters. She's the skinny one with auburn hair. If so, you can give her this." She plunked the napkin down by the register. "The posters can go in back, beside my desk, please."

"No problemo," Jen said with a smile. "You have fun out there."

Sam gathered her backpack, her folder of notes pertaining to the vendors, along with a tape measure and blank notepad.

The Bella Vista Hotel had once been a Taos showplace, with a driveway that swept up to a sturdy adobe porte-cochere, acres of manicured lawns and ancient cottonwood trees that thrived on the moisture from the Rio Fernando running behind the property. The design was Southwest-meets-Art-Deco, where a lobby with high ceiling formed the perfect focal point as one approached. Two-story wings flanked this central feature, rooms designed so that each small balcony had privacy plus a view of either the river, the gardens or the woods.

Over the years motel chains had come to town, eclipsing the classy old grand dame with their closer proximity to the middle of town, plentifully mundane rooms and cheaper prices. The Bella Vista had gone through hard times but kept its integrity as a place for the genteel and the art set. In times past it had claimed such luminaries as Georgia O'Keefe and D.H. Lawrence as guests. Rupert, as a member of that crowd, had no doubt called in some kind of favor in order to get the owners to allow the chocolate festival. Sam couldn't honestly remember there ever being such a public event here.

She parked in a lot that was discreetly screened from view by a row of high arbor vitae, consulted her notes and went in search of Auguste Handler, the manager. As it turned out, he stood behind the hotel's front desk, watching over the shoulder of a young clerk as the girl typed at a keyboard. Handler could have been anywhere between thirty and fifty, with perfectly trimmed dark hair, a pudgy face, and impeccably aligned ultra-white teeth. His dark suit seemed more in line with the attire of a metro male lawyer than a small town manager in the hospitality field, but apparently the outfit was in keeping with the image the Bella Vista wanted to portray.

Sam introduced herself and didn't merely imagine the critical glance directed toward her white baker's jacket.

"I'd like to take some measurements in the ballroom," she told him, "and maybe you can show me the outdoor area we'll be using."

"I will take you out to the gardens first," he said, aiming his polite smile just a tad over her shoulder. Not exactly a warm and friendly kind of guy; maybe she should have brought Rupert with her to butter him up.

Handler led the way through a side door and down a cloistered walkway until they came to a wide, graveled path that bisected the spacious lawn.

"We must insist that foot traffic stay to the gravel and the walkways. It's nearly impossible to keep a lawn intact in these dry conditions, much less one that has been trampled to oblivion." He pointed to one narrow area where his criteria could be met.

Sam took in the layout, the sun directly overhead, the forbidden grassy spaces. To effectively guarantee that crowds of people wouldn't trample the landscaping, they would need to erect fences or ropes and put up signs. This didn't look promising.

"May I see the ballroom now?"

She followed him back to the heavy glass doors through which they'd come, then down a wide corridor. He paused at a set of carved wood doors that were easily twelve feet tall and pushed inward on one of them. The deco theme was prevalent here with parquet floors, metal and glass wall sconces, massive pillars and art-glass chandeliers. She could practically see dancers in long, flowing skirts whirling to an orchestral waltz.

Pulling out her tape measure, she held it up. "Mind if I take some measurements?"

He spread his arms, palms upward, in a be-my-guest manner. "I will be at the desk, if you have any questions."

Okay, she thought, stretching the tape along the north wall, where high windows were draped with gold silk swags. Making lines and jotting measurements on her notepad, she sketched out the rectangular room. Booths could easily line most of the four walls, except where exit doors came in on the south wall and a service door, probably to the kitchen, was tucked into a corner of the east wall. She could also place a row of vendors along the center of the room, with breaks for the large pillars.

The committee had planned on allowing forty vendors, wanting as much variety as possible and giving everyone who wanted to sell their products the chance to do so. No matter what she did, no more than twenty-five booths were going to fit into this room. She wandered back to the garden and stared out over the pathway and lawn. Overhead, the sun blazed down and Sam could envision chocolate creations running down the fronts of table skirts and onto the ground—customers buying nothing and unhappy vendors. A sure way for the festival to get bad reviews in the press and ill will from the populace. She felt a headache coming on.

Back inside, she contemplated the ballroom again. A standard booth size was normally ten feet wide, but if she reworked that a bit and tweaked the placement . . . She called Kelly.

"How many vendors are signed up so far?"

"Twenty-three, I think." Pages rustled in the background. "Yep, that's it."

Sam stared at her sketch and made an executive decision. "Pull the ad calling for more, and tell anyone else who inquires that we're full."

Rather than taking on the agony of crowd control out there on the lawns, not to mention the grief she would get from vendors who didn't like their choice of site—indoors or out—she could simply limit the number to however many she could crowd into this room. That would be it. Double-checking her measurements, she paced off the booths and was even able to allow for a space at the west end of the room where they could erect a small platform to use for presentation of the prizes. The sponsor, *Qualitätsschokolade*, would be pleased to have that area for its advertisements.

She reviewed the sketch and felt satisfied. She would need to sit down with Kelly and go over the specific applications, decide placement of each booth, but at least this was a great start.

She found Auguste Handler—as promised—at the front desk.

"I think I have it all worked out and we'll only be using the ballroom, not the garden," she told him. "I will need access early Thursday morning, so I can mark off the vendor spaces. The vendors will begin setting up from noon onward that day."

He nodded, leaving a little expectant pause in the air.

"Ah, the check. I'll just—" Sam rummaged in her bag.

Handler stood there with the composed patience of his class, while Sam scribbled out the amount Rupert had told her. As she was ripping the check from her checkbook her phone rang. She pushed the check across the desk, thanked Mr. Handler and walked toward the exit as she pulled out her phone, noting that the call was from Sweet's Sweets.

Becky's voice was shaking so badly Sam could barely understand her.

"The pueblos—for the festival—"

"What's happened, Becky? Calm down."

But the explanation was incoherent.

"Hang on. I can be there in fifteen minutes," Sam said. She started her van and tried not to imagine too large a disaster awaiting her.

Chapter 5

Sam arrived at the bakery to find Julio working on one of the metal storage racks with a wrench, Becky sitting at Sam's desk with a cup of tea and red-rimmed eyes, and Jen picking up decorating tools and broken ceramic wedding cake toppers. Becky's eyes welled with tears when she saw Sam.

"Are you all right?" Sam rushed to her side and looked her over for injuries.

"I'm okay but I am *so* sorry! I don't know what happened."

Sam could pretty well figure it out. She'd been meaning to empty that rack and repair the shaky leg on it for some time. Since it meant unloading hundreds of little items and reorganizing the whole thing, she hadn't yet found a minute to do it.

Becky set her tea aside and stood up. "I just reached for the plastic bin with the bottles of edible glitter but that shelf was a bit over my head. I should have stood on a stool. This is the worst of it." She showed Sam the remains of the pueblo chocolates—some intact, many broken in pieces, lying among a litter of the small cardboard boxes in which they would have been sold.

A solid rock went to the pit of Sam's stomach. All that work. At home she might have claimed the five-second-rule and picked them up, but there was no way she could sell these in her business. Her license would be gone in moments even though the bakery floor was probably cleaner than in most hospitals.

"Let's see if any of the boxes can be salvaged," she said. "Unfortunately, the chocolate has to go."

A vision of the wooden box flashed through her head. In times past, faced with insurmountable deadlines, she had used its energy burst to perform some amazing things. But none of the employees knew that. She had to go carefully here.

"I'll come in at night and help with it," Becky pleaded. "Anything at all. I feel so awful."

Sam faced her and put her hands on Becky's shoulders. "It's not your fault. I should have fixed that shelf a long time ago. And I shouldn't have started stacking the chocolates there. I could have found a safer place."

Tears spilled down her assistant's face.

"Listen—it's fine. I've really got the recipe down pat now so I can remake them in a lot less time. Do not worry! I mean it."

Julio set down his wrench and gave the leg of the shelf a couple of good tugs. Sam went to his side and the two of them set the shelving unit upright. She gripped both sides of it and shook it. The thing felt solid but she agreed with Julio's suggestion that they should fasten it to the wall. He rummaged through her toolbox and came up with enough sturdy bolts to do the job.

"Okay, back to work," Sam said. "What else needs to be finished this afternoon?"

Becky pointed to a princess-themed birthday cake she'd been working on when the need for the glitter arose. She assured Sam that she felt steady enough to finish it. Jen went back to the front displays, and Sam began sorting through the boxes for clean, unbroken pueblo chocolates.

It would be far simpler to sell them from a bulk tray and bag them for the customers rather than boxing them in charming sets of four and six as she'd done earlier. She glanced at the clock. Tonight was as good a time as any; once the shop closed she would sneak back and work on them.

"Don't forget all these posters," Jen said later, as she set the bank bag on Sam's desk. She tilted her head toward a large box that Sam hadn't noticed earlier, what with the demands of reorganizing the contents of the downed shelf.

Carinda had, as per the plan, counted out some posters to place around town but had left the majority to be divided and distributed by Sam, since most of the committee members were her friends. She'd figured on twenty posters per person. Sam pulled a few off the stack and asked Jen to place two in the front windows of Sweet's Sweets and take twenty to Riki's dog grooming shop for distribution. She would see that Kelly took a share of them too. And she could drop by Rupert's place on her way home and leave a batch with him. Only forty or fifty to go—goody.

She carried the box out to her van, figuring she would ask everyone she came across to take a few. Beau might even be able to put them in the public areas around the sheriff's department and the county courthouse. With less than a week to go, they really needed to get these things posted soon around town.

Feeling a little lucky that neither Kelly nor Rupert were home when she got to their places, Sam left the posters where they would be found—in the kitchen at Kelly's and on a small tea table on Rupert's covered front porch. She got back into her van and drove away, wishing she was merely going home to crawl into bed early.

Unfortunately, her list of tasks was way too long and she didn't dare put off redoing the chocolates. The upcoming week could only get more crazy with each passing day.

She had no sooner pulled into the driveway than her phone sent out a trill that meant a text message from Beau: Traffic accident call—don't wait dinner.

Poor deluded husband—as if there would have been any dinner tonight anyway. She replied with a chipper tone, saying it was okay, she would catch up on some things at work. She parked beside the big log house where both dogs met her with such enthusiasm that she wished she really was going to stay home with them. She scooped food into their bowls and went upstairs in search of her magic energy fix.

The carved wooden box sat near the sink in the large master bathroom, right where she had left it. The sight of it reminded her that she really had meant to get back to the hospital to check on Sarah Williams. With luck, maybe her previous visit had helped Sarah improve to the point where she would soon go home. She picked up the box and closed her eyes, sending positive messages out to her friend as the warmth of the wood permeated her hands. The box's energy traveled up her arms; the moment her hands began to feel too hot she set it on the vanity top.

Shaking her arms to dispel the tingle, she made her plan—stop by the hospital to see Sarah, then back to the bakery to work on chocolates.

* * *

The parking lot at Holy Cross was packed with early evening visitors. Sam cruised through it twice and ended up parking on the street a half-block away. Inside, people hovered around the doorways of rooms that were too small to accommodate the large families who believed lots of bedside company was the cure for anything. The space around Sarah's room at the end of the hall was noticeably quiet. Sam peered inside to find the bed empty. Oh, no. She spun around to see a nurse walking toward her.

"Sarah Williams? Where is she?" Hoping like crazy she'd gone home.

"I'm afraid Ms. Williams slipped into a coma this afternoon. We've moved her to ICU." Seeing Sam's stricken expression, the nurse gave directions. Sam made her way to the wing with the glass-fronted rooms full of beeping equipment.

Marc Williams stood looking down at Sarah, who seemed even smaller and more defenseless than ever. Sam walked in, ignoring a nurse at the desk who seemed ready to ask questions.

"It happened pretty suddenly while I was gone to get

some lunch," Marc told her. "There is some bleeding in the brain and the doctors are deciding when to do surgery."

"Can I hold her hand for a minute?" she asked with a lump in her throat.

"I'm sure that would be all right." He moved aside and Sam stepped to the side of the bed that had fewer wires and tubes.

She took Sarah's hand and willed some of her excess energy through the connection between them. *Please get better, Sarah. Please come back.* It seemed selfish to end the thought by begging for the story of the other wooden box, the one in Ireland, but the idea did flash through her head for a split second.

Sarah stirred slightly but didn't blink or make a sound. After a couple of minutes Sam set her hand gently down on the blanket. She gave Marc her phone number and asked him to call if there was any change.

All the way to her shop, Sam thought of Sarah. They'd grown close during their work on the committee, laughing at Carinda's hysterics. Already she was missing Sarah's contributions to the meetings. And, she'd learned a lot about the wooden box and its previous owner from the older woman, but there was still so much more. What Sam knew must be only a fraction of the artifact's history; plus, the second box still intrigued her. She'd had the chance to hold it briefly, when she and Beau honeymooned in Ireland last year. She'd gotten no reaction from that one, nothing like she experienced every time she picked up hers. But still . . . there were so many unknowns. Her uncle Terry had promised to tell her the story—then he died. Now Sarah, who had hinted that Bertha might have said more about it. If Sarah died now, without saying anything more, did it mean that the second box carried some kind of curse? Something that prevented its secrets from being revealed?

No! Sam shook her head to clear this line of thought. Granted, Uncle Terry had owned and handled the other box, but she had learned nothing to suggest that either Bertha or Sarah ever actually came in contact with it. She had to stop this thinking and put her energy into something practical, such as replacing the ruined chocolates.

She parked behind the shop and let herself into the quiet kitchen. Her supply of dark cacao was running low and she had to do some quick adjustments to the recipe. How much simpler this would be if Bobul, that oddball chocolatier, were to show up and take over. The large man in the heavy brown coat, with his bag of mysterious ingredients and tools, always made the entire chocolate-making process seem so effortless.

She pulled out her largest kettle, feeling brave about tackling one large batch rather than making smaller ones as she'd been doing. She carefully weighed the sugar and butter and began stirring the mixture over a low flame on the stovetop.

Within minutes the familiar motions of stirring and watching the ingredients blend calmed her. She sent her remaining energy through the handle of the spoon and into the bubbling pot. The chocolate took on a creamy quality the moment she added pinches of those little powders Bobul had given her. Whatever was in those pouches, it was *the* thing that made her chocolates special, gave them qualities unlike any other. When the mixture was perfect she poured it out for tempering, working automatically and quickly.

Filling the pueblo molds didn't use nearly all of the dark mixture, so she pulled out every other mold she owned.

Any shape that didn't specifically scream 'Christmas' got put to use, as Sam turned out flowers, stars, shells and generic shapes. She placed the molds on trays in the cooling racks and looked around, feeling the last of her residual energy drain away.

The chocolate-coated kettle sat in the sink; sticky spoons and spatulas lay about, but it was only ten o'clock. She had fully expected to work through the night. She gathered the tools and dumped them all into the large pot, squirted detergent on top and filled the thing with hot water. The actual scrubbing could wait until morning, she decided, turning out the lights and locking the back door.

The ranch looked so good, the porch light glowing softly to welcome her home, the dogs sitting expectantly on the porch unable to settle down until their 'pack' was complete. She pulled the van into her normal spot and greeted Ranger and Nellie, who herded her toward the front door. Beau greeted them and led Sam to the kitchen where he brewed a cup of her favorite tea.

"Long day, huh?"

"I swear that eighty percent of my day goes toward this dumb festival right now. One more week and I plan to give myself an extra day or two off."

His eyes wandered upward. "You must have been tired when you stopped in earlier. You forgot your phone. I think you have a few messages."

"Oh, god. Not tonight."

Upstairs, she found the phone on the bed where she had changed shoes at some point in the afternoon. No way was she going to make calls this late at night, and she knew better than to listen to the voicemail messages because something on there would surely rob her of her sleep.

Better to find out in the morning. She turned off the ringer and stowed the phone deep inside her pack before heading to the shower.

By five a.m. Sam had brewed coffee when Beau came downstairs, ready for his day in uniform.

"Well, the Flower People have started to show up," he said, pouring the hot brew into his favorite mug.

"Oh, honey, last night I was so tired I completely forgot to ask how your day went. I'm sorry." Sam put her arms around him. "How's it going with them?"

"As of dusk yesterday, there were two old converted school buses, painted blue, with about a dozen occupants. They passed me on the road and I watched them turn off at Mulvane's place."

"Maybe you'll get lucky and that's all there will be."

He snorted. "I really doubt that but I will try to hold on to your positive attitude."

"And meanwhile I bet you are cruising by there all day long to keep an eye on things."

"The old 'trust but verify'? Except in this case I have very little trust." He seemed restless. "Can I take you out to breakfast?"

Sam thought of the eight voicemail messages she was avoiding, all from festival committee members. "Absolutely. Anything to delay leaping into the fray."

"How about that little burrito place out by the ski valley turnoff? You can ride with me and then I'll bring you back here to get your van."

"And this choice would have nothing to do with the fact that we'll drive right by Mulvane's place on the way."

"Okay, you got me." He plucked his Stetson off the bentwood rack near the front door.

Sam stuffed her phone into her pocket, leaving her backpack and the folder of festival notes on the kitchen table.

Beau steered down their long driveway in the department cruiser and made a right turn at the road, away from town. A quarter mile farther, the narrow lane leading to the neighboring ranch showed fresh tracks in the dusty earth. Two rural mailboxes sat on posts near the turnoff, one being Mulvane's and the other belonging to Max Rodriguez whose land was accessed by this same dirt road. Beau made the turn, moving slowly.

The Mulvane house, a faux-adobe structure, sat beyond a wide green metal gate of the county-issue variety, accessed by a skinny driveway that led directly to the attached garage. In the opposite direction, following the fence line, new tracks went westbound. A fallow dirt field now sported four buses.

"Looks like more of them arrived after dark," Beau commented.

Sam noticed two campfires where women in long skirts hunkered down to stir something in pots. Three naked children ran by, shrieking at each other, undeterred by the chill in the morning air. A bearded man outside one of the buses ran his fingers through long hair, stretched mightily, and turned his back on Beau's SUV.

Beau drove past the encampment and used a wide spot in the lane beyond Mulvane's house to turn around.

"I count at least twenty people now," he said as they passed the buses again.

Sam kept quiet but before they reached the highway a small procession led by a battered VW van met them head-on. She felt Beau's tension edge up three notches.

Chapter 6

The breakfast burrito lay heavily in her stomach as Beau drove away and Sam let herself into the house. Beau had spent the time dispatching a couple of deputies to cruise the area a few times a day. Meanwhile, her phone had vibrated twice during their meal and she knew there was no escaping the obligation; it would be best to deal with the calls before her workday at the bakery began. She sat at the table with a notepad and started listening to messages.

Auguste Handler: "Ms. Sweet, I understood that your group planned to use only the ballroom? Your associate now informs me that you also need the garden area. The fee will be different, you understand. Call me, please."

Harvey Byron: "Sam, what's this all about? I'm supposed to sell ice cream outdoors, with no access to electricity to keep my refrigeration running? Call me ASAP."

An unknown female voice: "Ms. Sweet, this is Farrel O'Hearn in Santa Fe. My assigned vendor location at Sweet Somethings simply will not do. Please call me with a reassignment."

Marc Williams: "Sam, sorry to bother you. You asked for updates on Aunt Sarah's condition, and I just wanted to let you know they've taken her into surgery. No need to call back. I'm going to my hotel for some sleep. I would like to speak with you later, if possible."

Auguste Handler: "Ms. Sweet, I haven't heard from you yet. A wedding party wants the garden. Since our contract calls for only your use of the ballroom . . . Please call me. Soon."

Rupert: "Sam . . .? Where are you? Pick up? Carinda Carter is driving me nuts!"

Carinda: "Sam, hi. Just wanted to let you know that I've got everything under control. No worries whatsoever. Talk to you soon. Bye."

Sam dropped her pen and held her head in her hands.

"I hate dealing with *people*!" She moaned it so loudly that Nellie the border collie came over and laid her chin on Sam's thigh. It's okay, the dog seemed to say.

"Nellie, it's not okay. This stupid chocolate fair is going to drive me insane."

She glanced over the names again. There had to be a way to prioritize them. Since Auguste Handler had the power to completely shut them down, she hit the redial button beside his name.

"Ms. Carter said she was on your committee and that she was in charge of organizing the vendor booths," he said after Sam basically asked what the hell was going on. "She came by, probably a half-hour after you left. Sketched out both the garden and ballroom layouts and said the festival would be needing both locations after all. To accommodate that I will require another five hundred dollars."

Sam willed her voice to stay calm. "Okay, first, Carinda Carter was not put in charge of the vendor booths."

"But—"

"I don't care what she said. We're taking the ballroom, that's it."

"So I can let this wedding party use the garden on Sunday?"

"Yes. And if you should hear from Carinda Carter again, don't discuss anything with her. Refer her back to me. Please."

He seemed a little put out about all the extra communication, but he wasn't the only one. She dialed Harvey, who seemed among the least antagonistic in his message.

"Check your email, Sam. She drew up a diagram of the hotel, marked off spaces and told each of us where our booths would be. I didn't know she was supposed to do that. I specifically said on my application that I would need to be near an electrical outlet."

"I know, Harvey. I had no idea Carinda was doing this. I have another map and you are definitely near a wall plug."

Relief was evident in his voice when he thanked her and hung up. She dialed Rupert next—might as well leap right back into the drama.

"What's going on?" she asked innocently enough.

"Didn't the committee meet only two days ago? How is it that Hurricane Carinda managed so much damage so quickly?" From the high tone in his voice, Sam could picture him striding around his writing room.

"I'm getting calls from all over. Farrel O'Hearn, who thinks her you-know-what doesn't stink has expressly forbid Carinda from contacting her, for any reason. And I'm the one who got the earful."

"What's she done?"

"In Farrel's words, 'I'll bring this festival down if my booth isn't the first one people see as they walk through the door. *I* studied at Ecole au Chocolat, the finest school in *Paris*. There is *no one* who will either make or break your little county fair the way I will'."

Sam had to laugh at the way Rupert captured the accent and intonation of the voice she'd heard in O'Hearn's high-toned message.

"Is she really that important?" she asked.

"I'd say she's semi-important. She's a Santa Fe snob and could probably badmouth us among that crowd. However, I know a lot of that same group and, believe me, I can play tit-for-tat with the best of them."

"Okay, well, let's don't go there yet. I can do something to appease her, I'm sure."

"You don't have to suck up, Sammy. I can deal with Farrel O'Hearn."

"For now, don't do anything. Please, Rupe, you don't know how full my hands are at this moment."

He grumbled a little but agreed to let it go. Sam looked at her diagram, shuffled a couple of things and penciled Farrel O'Hearn into one of the center spaces. When she called, the woman tried the high-handed approach and Sam let her rant for a good three minutes before informing her that the site diagram had been sent by mistake. When

O'Hearn heard the booth number of her new spot she gave a grudging thanks, as if the prime location was her due all along, and hung up. Sam scratched a heavy line through her name on the phone call list.

Her next call wouldn't be fun but it was important to address quickly. Carinda sounded a little surprised by Sam's abrupt tone and agreed to meet her at Sweet's Sweets at one o'clock.

"Do not contact any vendor or committee member until we've talked," Sam said. She punctuated the request by hanging up.

I hate this, I hate this, I hate this! Managing people and coordinating an event were definitely not her forte. For a moment she thought fondly back to the days when all she had to do was bake the occasional birthday cake for a kid's party and then go break into a house or two, easy work that she could perform by herself.

She dialed Kelly next. "I'll be at the bakery in about twenty minutes. Can you set aside some time to meet me there and help with something?"

Another flash from the past, the time not that many years ago when she could measure her daughter's reliability in nanometers. Thankfully, they had come a long way since.

Kelly apparently heard the van drive up because she stepped out the back door of Puppy Chic before Sam got out of her vehicle.

"Hey, thanks. Riki was okay with your taking a few minutes off?"

"No prob. She's bathing an Irish Setter, which will take her longer than this job will take us."

Sam led the way directly to her desk and pulled up an extra chair.

"Okay, here's my diagram of the floor plan. I've marked the ones I've assigned already. If you can take this stack of applications and find the ones with special requests— like if they require electricity or can't be near the windows or something like that. We'll assign them first and then fit everyone else in. Try not to put similar products right next to each other. We'll have battles if all the cookies are in one section and all the cakes in another. Space them out."

"Got it."

Within twenty minutes they had a workable plan that included the promises she'd made earlier.

"Now, Kel, if you can scan this and email it out to all the vendors, I will be eternally grateful. If none of them get back in my face we'll officially deem it a miracle and your place in heaven is assured."

Kelly laughed and took over at the computer keyboard.

Sam took a moment to check in with each of her employees and assure herself that there were no bakery disasters lurking unseen. Her molded chocolates from last night were waiting safely in the cooling racks; she got out the last of the small decorative boxes and began creating assortments. The remaining ones could be sold individually.

"All done," Kelly said a few minutes later, on her way out the back door. She snagged a brownie from a tray that Julio was about to carry to the front.

Sam smiled. "Thanks."

"Oh! I meant to tell you, Mom, I met up with Sarah Williams's next door neighbor—one of the ladies who was helping with the decorations? We went to Sarah's, where they'd been working together and I loaded everything into my car. I'll take it all to the hotel when we get ready to set up."

"You're a peach."

Kelly's eyebrows pulled together. "I have to say, the place was pretty messy. For Sarah, I mean. That time I stopped by to give her a ride—I tell you, the lady could have won some kind of good housekeeping award. This time there were drawers and cabinet drawers hanging open . . . not at all tidy."

Hm. Sam agreed with Kelly's assessment of Sarah's housekeeping style and this was not normal. Marc must have had a hard time locating those insurance documents. She waved Kelly out the back and went back to work.

She'd boxed about half of the chocolates when the familiar roar of a truck sounded outside the door and the brown-uniformed UPS guy peered in.

"Several big cartons for you, Sam. Where shall I put them?"

Big cartons? She hadn't ordered anything recently.

"I better take a look," she said, wiping her hands on a towel and following him out to the alley.

At the back of his big, square truck sat three boxes that were taller than she, all with the *Qualitätsschokolade* logo. What on earth—?

The driver was looking at her expectantly.

"Uh, wow . . ." There was no way they would fit inside the bakery without being in everyone's way. Her own booth tables and display cases were already taking a huge amount of space. The barn at home came to mind. But without dismantling the shelving inside her bakery van she couldn't use it to transport them. She would have to go home for her pickup truck. She chewed at her lip for a moment.

"I guess just leave them here in the alley for now, right by my door. I'll think of something." Something that didn't involve curious thieves or an overeager garbage truck driver.

"For their size, they aren't too heavy," said the driver as he manipulated a hand truck under the edge of one. The carton threatened to tip as he struggled to wheel it. "Just bulky."

Sam signed for the delivery then pulled out her phone and dialed Beau.

"Where are you right now?" she asked.

"At my desk, catching up on department paperwork."

"Want a break from it?" She explained her dilemma. "I can run home and get the truck myself, but I'll still need help maneuvering these things."

"Tell you what. I'll drive home and get your truck, bring it back and help you."

"Really, I didn't mean for you to take that much time . . ."

"It'll give me the chance to take a peek at what's going on out that direction, see how many more buses and vans have shown up."

She hung up, hoping he wouldn't become too distracted before they could get these boxes out of the alley. Meanwhile, Becky needed worktable space for a large multi-tiered cake so Sam rushed back inside to get the rest of the molded chocolates put away.

Beau's expression seemed a little grim when he pulled up forty-five minutes later. He gripped one of the large cartons and practically flung it into the bed of Sam's truck.

"Wait, Beau! You'll strain something lifting like that." She rushed to his side and together they picked up the next one.

"What's the matter?" she asked, feeling slightly winded

after keeping up with his long strides.

"Nothing, I hope. But there's a steady stream of old vans, beater cars and other junk vehicles traveling the road toward our place. There must be well over a hundred camping out on Mulvane's property by now."

Oh boy.

They placed the third big carton into the truck and she climbed into the passenger seat. He drove carefully through the back streets of town, keeping an eye on the bulky boxes. When they came to the red light at Camino de la Placita, they counted twelve more vehicles that clearly belonged to the hippie enclave.

"And this isn't counting the ones driving in from other directions, coming out of Colorado and across the western part of the state."

She could see why he wasn't terribly happy about the visitors. "Did old man Mulvane know there would be so many?"

"I have no idea. My guess is that the lure of their money overshadowed any details he should have asked for."

"So, is there some way to overturn that contract he signed?"

"Well, the process would involve getting a restraining order or a stay against them, while we try to prove that Mr. Mulvane wasn't competent to enter such an agreement. I would have to give some proof of why he might be considered incompetent. Best I could hope for would be a sympathetic judge who might put them off for awhile."

They had joined the slow-moving line of traffic now. It really was sounding complicated.

"In Colorado, the neighbors had no luck in overturning

the contract last year. The Flower People most likely will be gone before we could complete the process."

"Maybe they'll only stay through the weekend." She worked toward a hopeful tone but remembered that he'd said these guys often remained for months. It wasn't looking like a great start to the summer.

At their turnoff, Sam noticed that he'd left his department cruiser parked near the road, in plain view of the passing traffic. It was probably one reason the line of cars moved along at a crawl. He drove the truck up the driveway and past the house, backing up to the double-wide barn doors where they both hopped out and quickly stashed the boxes against the front of an unused horse stall.

"What's in these things anyway?" he asked as they set the last one down.

"I have no idea. I guess I should ask Rupert. He's the one who made the deal with this Swiss chocolate company to sponsor the festival."

"My guess," Rupert said when she called him on the way back to her shop, "it's probably their display materials. I can come over and help you unpack it. Ooh—it'll be like Christmas!"

Sam glanced at her dashboard clock. She actually could turn around and get back home pretty quickly, but Carinda would be showing up at the shop within the hour. She told Rupert they better get to the boxes later in the afternoon.

She and Becky were in the middle of checking inventory for the festival—there were more than a dozen boxes filled with brownies, cookies, filled croissants and cupcakes. She also planned on having her secret recipe amaretto cheesecake for sale by the slice and a couple of the deep chocolate

Kahlua cakes. The task now was to count everything and be sure the supplies were adequate.

Tomorrow, while Sam set up the venue and directed the other vendors as they arrived on site, Becky and Julio would continue to bake whatever items might run low. If the first day was a sellout, both of her bakers had committed to work Saturday to assure more stock for the final day.

"That's the plan," she told Becky after reciting it all.

"And you know what they say about the best laid plans." Becky grinned as she carried two boxes of brownies back to the fridge.

"Sam?" Jen had walked up behind her and Sam jumped when her assistant touched her shoulder. "That Carinda Carter is here."

Sam braced herself. She needed to be firm with Carinda about her duties but she also remembered how easily the woman's feelings had been hurt at the last committee meeting. She walked into the showroom to find Carinda facing her, birdlike legs in a firm stance, skinny arms planted on her almost non-existent hips.

"You have something to say to me?" Carinda demanded.

Chapter 7

Excuse me?" Sam said.
        "You have a lot of nerve, lecturing me." Carinda came forward, shaking her index finger at Sam.

Sam glanced toward Jen, who stood frozen behind the register. A customer who had been browsing the cookie selection edged toward the front of the room.

"Carinda, how about if we discuss this outside? A little stroll might help."

Sam walked to the front door and held it open, ready to step out and leave Carinda talking to the walls unless she followed. Leading the way past the front of Puppy Chic, Sam started out with the gentle tone she'd planned to use.

"Carinda, I want you to know that we all appreciate—"

"Like hell! No one has cared one bit for all the work I put in. I had those booth spaces lined up perfectly—then I find out you redid all my work according to some other plan that didn't even exist!"

"Carinda—"

"I have to do everything for this festival and then you come along and—"

Sam stopped in the middle of the sidewalk. "Wait just a minute. It was never your assignment to allocate the booth spaces. I'm not saying that you couldn't have done it, but you didn't have the vendor applications and didn't know what each of them needed."

"And what about distributing the posters all over town? That was another of my jobs that someone else took over. I tell you, I'm mad as hell over this!" She spun toward Sam. "And then you *dared* to hang up on me."

Sam felt the sting of that—she had done so.

"Sorry. Can't we just—"

"I'm not putting up with it. I don't need any of you people. I might as well just—" Her eyes were wild and she made a hacking motion with her hand.

"Carinda, settle down. That's crazy talk." Sam reached to touch her shoulder but the woman jerked back and ran toward her car.

"Crazy? You think I'm crazy?" She yanked open the car door and slid in, starting the engine and putting the car in gear immediately. "Well, *you* are a controlling bitch!" she shouted through her open window.

Sam stood frozen to the spot. Crazy? That would probably be a yes.

"Sam? What's going on?" Riki had stepped out of her grooming shop with a tiny Maltese cradled in her arms, just in time to hear the chirp of Carinda's tires and the honk of another driver's horn when she reached the street.

"I have no idea."

Riki shrugged and gave the fluffy white dog a tickle on its head before going back inside.

Why did I go for the bait? Sam chided herself on the way back to Sweet's Sweets. *I knew the lady was a little off balance; why didn't I pacify her?*

Because maybe everyone has always pacified her and that's how she gets away with these temper tantrums. Or, she's having raging PMS?

Another car had pulled up in front of the bakery and a woman with two kids got out. Sam held the door, then followed them inside where she sent Jen a half smile and continued to the back.

"Trouble?" Becky asked, looking up from a tray of chocolate nut drop cookies.

"I really hope our voices didn't carry all the way in here."

"Only a comment or two when your visitor first arrived."

Sam rolled her eyes. Four more days and she would never have to speak to Carinda Carter again. The image of that slashing motion came back to her—could Carinda be suicidal? Maybe she shouldn't be so flippant about this. She supposed one never knew with someone whose moods swung as wildly as this woman's. Maybe she could learn something more about Carinda's state of mind from Rupert when they met to unpack the boxes in the barn.

Sam couldn't get Carinda's freaky mood swings out of her mind as she finished checking her festival inventory, gave a glance at her desk and informed the others that she would make a couple of deliveries and would be at home after that.

She phoned Rupert as she was leaving the home of a baby shower hostess, where a cupcake tree featuring two dozen pink booties was now ready for a party. He agreed to be out at the ranch in twenty minutes.

"Never saw the woman before that first committee meeting," Rupert said when she brought up Carinda's odd behavior.

Sam unlocked the barn and swung the big door open. Late afternoon shadows made the place a little gloomy but high windows at each end gave enough light for their purposes.

"I was under the impression she knew Sarah Williams or that somebody else at the Chamber of Commerce had talked her into volunteering," he said as Sam showed him inside.

The mention of Sarah's name reminded Sam that a couple of days had passed in a blur and she'd heard nothing new from Marc Williams. She should give him a call this evening.

"Whoa, look at this!" Rupert had slit open one of the tall, flat boxes and he now peeled back the top to reveal an elegantly printed panel with the *Qualitätsschokolade* logo overlaid across a superb hi-def photo showing bricks of chocolate.

Together they lifted the panel to reveal another. The other flat box contained two more. The set of four were designed to snap together for a booth backdrop.

"They told me they would send some colorful advertising materials. This will be perfect in the dais area you set aside for the judging, Sam. I can see our celebrity judges sitting in front of this beauty."

Sam had slit the tape on a large cube-shaped box. Cloth banners of the same royal blue used in the corporate logo would drape elegantly above the scrumptious photos.

"Look." She held out a roll of stickers, small enough

to go on vendor badges and to be given out to kids who roamed the festival. "And . . . goodie bags for the vendors! What a great idea, including recipe ideas using their various chocolates. Everyone will love these."

Rupert was poking around in the box, like a kid with his Christmas stocking. "Chocolate truffles," he said. "I recognize these; they're one of the more exclusive Swiss brands. There's a huge box of them. We can give them out to everyone who stops by the judging stand."

"And these . . ." Sam held up gift-bagged mugs with packets of hot chocolate mix. ". . . these will make great door prizes. People hang around longer if they might win a prize. Rupert, this is so cool. How can I ever thank you enough for finding this sponsor?"

He actually looked a little bit humble. "Well, you are letting me do some sneaky promotion for my secret nom de plume."

"Speaking of promotion, I'm making you and Bentley the MCs of this deal. You work out the timing for prize drawings and coordinate the tastings so the judges get around to all the entries."

Sam thought again of Sarah, sad that she wasn't here to enjoy the festivities. After all, she'd been the one to start the ball rolling for the festival in the first place.

Rupert had stacked the photo panels neatly so they would fit in the back of Sam's pickup when it came time to take them to the hotel ballroom.

"I can take the prizes and other small items with me now," he offered. "If you want some of these things out of your hair."

"Anything. Take any and all of it that you wish." *See,*

Carinda? I'm not a controlling bitch.

Carinda really *had* gotten to her this afternoon. Sam wanted to drop it but couldn't let go of that image of the rail-thin woman stomping back to her car, throwing insults as she went. The woman was over-the-top batty, and the sooner this whole event was over, the better.

Beau pulled into the long driveway just as Rupert was driving out. He walked over to the open barn door and Sam showed him the display materials they had just unboxed.

"Pretty amazing, huh? I think our little festival is taking on a really professional tone."

He nodded with a grunt.

"Beau?"

"Grr. It's Mulvane. Now he's calling my department, a little worried that so many of the Flower People are showing up. It's getting out of hand, he says, and he wants me to supply a security detail."

"Can you even do that?" She watched as he swung the barn door into place and latched it.

"I pointed out to him that no one is breaking the law, and that it was only a few days ago he was chasing me off his land, saying he had the right to do whatever he wanted. I told him to call a private security firm if he wanted to."

"And?"

"Well, now it comes out that the earth children only gave him five hundred dollars, with a promise of more before they go. He can't afford much in the way of hired security for that."

They walked to the house, where Sam pulled two beer bottles from the fridge.

"It's always this way," he said, taking his. "People get

themselves in trouble and then expect public resources to bail them out. The fool who tried to parachute off the gorge bridge awhile back, got his lines twisted, and State Police had to get a helicopter out there and a rescue team to pull him back. All those out-of-shape hikers each year who start up the mountain wearing sneakers and then need Search and Rescue to come after them when they've slid off a rock and broken their legs. They're lucky if they don't die but do they ever pay for those services? No."

"Do you think Mr. Mulvane is genuinely afraid of the hippies?"

"Nah. I think one or two of them may have mouthed off to him, but generally they seem to be of the 'peace and love' set. His wife may have gotten pretty offended when she observed a trio doing the 'love' part of it behind one of the buses in full daylight. I think that's what's behind this sudden desire to have some uniforms around."

"So, what's your plan?"

"I'll go out there in the morning and talk to them, just let them know that there are eyes everywhere and that we expect everything to stay quiet and legal."

"Let's hope. Meanwhile, since we're both in for the evening, how about if we grill some burgers?"

He gave her a kiss, thanked her for being the voice of reason, and went outside to light the grill. Sam went to the fridge and pulled out lettuce and tomatoes, the ground beef and some onion rolls she'd bought a few days ago. She worked automatically, assembling the meal, but Carinda Carter's parting words kept nagging at her. Tomorrow, she would see Carinda as they set up the ballroom for the festival. Not looking forward to that.

She fell asleep by telling herself that nothing on her

crowded agenda could be accomplished in the middle of the night and that she would awaken in the morning with renewed energy to deal with it all. Good in theory, but she woke up at three-thirty and nothing would make those eyes close again. She tiptoed around the bedroom and bathroom, getting dressed as quietly as possible, and left Beau snoring peacefully.

By the time she arrived at the Bella Vista at nine o'clock she had already spent nearly five hours at Sweet's Sweets where she had baked another four-dozen brownies for her booth and while they were in the oven she'd decorated one of this weekend's wedding cakes. She drove past the hotel's elegant entrance and parked in the same lot as before, noting that Rupert's vehicle was the only one she recognized.

Sure enough, the big man was there in what he would consider work clothes—soft grey cashmere pants and a breezy purple tunic. His silver hair flowed straight back from his forehead to his shirt collar, with teeth marks from his comb, although those would go away as soon as it fully dried.

"Please appreciate the fact that I have taken away from my sacrosanct writing time this morning for this project," he said, grazing her cheek with a kiss.

"I do, Rupe. You're the best."

"So, what's first, lady-boss?"

She stared around the cavernous ballroom. "Here's my sketch. We need to measure off the booth spaces and put masking tape on the floor so everyone knows the boundaries."

"Good idea. Never trust people to agree over territory."

They began near the corner door that led to the kitchen, measuring and marking their way down the north wall, then the west. Kelly showed up at some point, explaining that Riki needed to keep her shop open and wouldn't be coming.

"At least she gave me the whole morning off. Just let me know what to do."

"Take Rupert's end of the tape measure," Sam said. "He's going to bring in some displays from my truck and start setting up the judging area."

"Ooh, the judges!" Kelly said. "Is Bentley Day here yet?"

"He's supposed to arrive this afternoon. We got a room comp'd for him here at the hotel."

Harvey Byron arrived, followed soon after by Carinda who fluttered around like an annoying moth, mainly in the way, talking nonstop so she seemed busy. Sam handed her roll of masking tape over to Harvey and took Carinda out to the corridor.

"Are you doing all right today?" she asked.

Carinda's eyebrows pulled together in puzzlement. "Sure, just fine."

"I just . . . Look, before the festival really gets underway, I want to apologize for letting things get a bit ugly yesterday. I shouldn't have been so sharp in my tone."

"I don't know what you mean."

"Well, you seemed really upset. I didn't intend to do that."

Again, the blank look. Did Carinda truly not remember acting as if she might do away with herself? Or was she such a drama queen that those types of moves were simply part of her normal repertoire? The word 'crazy' popped into Sam's head again.

"All right. Whatever." Carinda shrugged. "I'd like to

start putting up the bunting and signs?"

"Let's get the booths numbered first, in case vendors start showing up early." She handed Carinda a stack of white pages on which she had printed large numbers, one through twenty-five. "Just follow Kelly and Harvey around and stick the numbers to the corresponding spaces they've taped off."

Sam didn't miss the resentful look Carinda sent her for being given the lowly task. *We're oil and water, that's all it is. We will never be friends but at least we can get through this weekend without a battle.* She repeated it to herself a couple more times.

At the south end of the room, two hotel employees had wheeled in sections of a portable platform and were in the process of noisily erecting it. Rupert looked a little impatient at the time it was taking to accomplish the task, but there was no point in putting up any of the decorative touches until the dais was in place. Sam walked over to be sure the men knew exactly where to place the heavy platform and accompanying access steps, then she took Rupert aside.

"Can I help you bring the rest of those promotional goodies inside?" she offered. "I could use a break from the racket."

The garden was a blanket of calm after the clamor of voices and assembly noise from the workmen indoors. They followed a walkway toward the parking lot.

"Slow down a little," Sam said, trying to keep up with Rupert's long stride. "These may be the last moments of calm that I get for the next three days."

He laughed and adjusted his pace to a saunter. They'd barely cleared the small rose garden when Sam's phone rang.

"Argh—even in a garden there's no peace," she said, reaching for it.

The number on the readout was unfamiliar, a local one. "Hello?"

"Sam, it's Marc Williams." His tone was not upbeat.

Her heart thudded, dreading bad news.

"My aunt has slightly come around. She spoke your name. Can you come to the hospital? Is this a good time?"

Well, the answer was that there would not be a good time all weekend, but for Sarah she would go anytime. She assured him she would get there as soon as possible.

Rupert caught the gist of it. "I'll handle the decorations, the committee, and all catastrophes. You go."

She left him in the parking lot and urged her truck toward the hospital at the other end of town, a sense of unease creeping over her.

Chapter 8

Behind the glass of the ICU room Sam could see activity, a nurse in a bright pink scrub top hovering around the bed. Marc Williams stood out in the hall, staring toward the monitors above his aunt's bed.

"What's going on?" Sam asked. "Is she still awake?"

He shook his head. "I don't know. She wasn't talking by the time I arrived but she raised her hand a little when I touched it. Then some kind of beeping thing went off and the nurse rushed in."

That didn't sound good. Sam stood beside him and watched, without knowing what she was seeing.

The nurse tucked Sarah's arm under the blanket and adjusted a dial on one of the machines before turning toward the door. She shook her head as she stepped out.

"Sorry, she's gone under again. I doubt she'll be talking

anytime soon, but you can certainly stay as long as you'd like."

Sam envisioned a long, silent wait by a bedside while all her other obligations piled up on her. She introduced herself to the nurse.

"Marc told me that Sarah spoke my name. Were you the nurse who was with her when she did that?"

The young woman nodded.

"Did she say anything at all, other than my name?"

"I'm afraid it was just 'Sam—is Sam here?' Her eyes were open and it came out clearly. She also asked who Marc was." The nurse shifted her gaze to the nephew. "I'm sorry it happened before you arrived. She might have responded better if she had seen you, but that's not always the case either."

She excused herself and walked toward her station.

Sam looked at Marc. Could there be reason for hope based on Sarah's brief revival?

"I know you are super busy right now," Marc said. "Aunt Sarah had told me about the festival and all. She was so excited about it. I wish she could be there."

"Me too. She really got us off to a good start." Sam felt the weight of sadness when she saw Sarah lying helplessly in the bed.

"Look, you don't have to hang around," he offered. "I'll stay awhile. I can call you right away if she wakes up again. If you want me to tell her anything about that box—?"

Sam was a little ashamed of the relief she felt but there really was no point in sitting here. She wasn't family and it was a wonder the medical staff had gone to so much trouble to accommodate her already.

"That's okay. Thanks. I really am swamped with this

event right now, but please do call me if there's a change. I would love to have another conversation with her. I'm going to keep positive thoughts in that direction. She'll recover and we will have lots of great talks."

Marc tried to look as if he believed that and Sam appreciated the brave face. She squeezed his hand and walked back out into the bright sunshine.

The big photographic panels for the *Qualitätsschokolade* booth were still in the back of her truck, she realized, protected only by their cardboard carton. Rupert had probably already missed them but refrained from interrupting her. She called him to say that she was on the way back then checked in with Beau to make sure he still had his sanity over the neighborhood situation. They agreed to try to meet for lunch, but no promises.

Sam arrived at the hotel to find that the makeup of the parking lot had changed entirely. Gone were the rental sedans and minivans with luggage carriers on top. Their spaces were now filled with trucks piled high with anonymous cardboard boxes, the spindly metal legs of trade show displays and sturdy folding tables. The vendors had arrived.

She called Rupert, suggesting that he grab a couple of able bodies and get outside. If they could meet her immediately she would triple park while they unloaded the photo displays. Otherwise, they were in for a long carry across the entire lot. She came to a stop near the garden walkway and Rupert, Kelly and Harvey appeared a few moments later.

"I probably need to assign someone to direct traffic out here," she said as they quickly pulled the large panels out of her truck. "Everyone who shows up this afternoon will have the same problem, and I can see Loading Zone issues if there isn't some kind of plan."

"Maybe the hotel can provide someone. I'll talk to the classy Mr. Handler," said Kelly.

"Thanks. It's okay if you bat those lashes at him a little." Sam drove away to park on the far side of the lot while the others maneuvered their load inside.

In a matter of under two hours the ballroom had changed from a spacious art-deco chamber to a chaos of clutter. Almost a third of the vendor spaces showed activity. Battered utility tables held boxes and bags; aluminum-framed structures marked delineations of territory and would eventually carry signage for the various businesses and individual exhibitors who planned to make their mark. Hard to believe that by tomorrow morning the huge room would be transformed to a magical world of chocolate. At the moment it had a *long* way to go.

The dais had been covered in blue carpeting, the front draped in a royal blue fabric skirt, and Rupert was standing back while Harvey and another man shifted the tall photographic panels into alignment. Throughout the room, conversations were punctuated by the occasional clatter of metal chairs or thump of heavy cartons.

"Bring that fourth one a little closer in. To your left," Rupert said as Sam approached. He turned to her. "What do you think? Do those look straight?"

"They're great."

With the panels in place, Rupert turned to the big carton of banners he'd brought. Kelly walked up as he began pawing through them.

"Mr. Handler has sent a couple of maintenance men

to oversee the parking situation," she said. "What else can I do?"

"If you and Harvey can set up that folding table," Rupert said, "we'll use these banners as draping. It's where the judges will be sitting while they taste the entries."

"I'll leave you to this," Sam told them, eyeing the spot where her own booth would be, next to Harvey's ice cream stand. Her space still held nothing but a numbered tag on the floor.

She pulled out her phone, intending to call the shop and make sure someone could break away soon to bring her display materials and help her get it organized. The actual baked products would come tomorrow morning in the van. She had tapped the first two digits of the number when she heard a familiar voice.

Ivan Petrenko, owner of the neighboring bookshop, stood beside her looking a little bewildered. "Good morning, Miss Samantha. Is good to be seeing you here."

Cute, how formally he always greeted her even though they had known each other for years.

"I am having some small problem, please. Where is to be finding my place?"

It always took Sam a second to figure out his curious mix of English and Russian phrasing. "Your booth? Let me check."

She consulted the clipboard that was beginning to feel like her third hand, and located the chart.

"You are in the center section, right next to Farrel O'Hearn, the master chocolatier from Santa Fe. I'll show you."

She led the way and saw that Farrel was already well

into the complicated setup she'd brought. Apparently, the woman planned some sort of demonstration since her equipment included two small vats and a stack of utensils. Her slender frame was already decked out in a flame-orange baker's jacket and black slacks, and her reddish hair sported a fresh cut that didn't look as if it could possibly wilt in the heat of a kitchen. Sam introduced her to Ivan and noticed that Farrel gave him the suspicious eye until it became clear that he only planned to sell books.

"I assume you have mine. It was a *New York Times* bestseller in 2002," Farrel said, gazing down her sharp nose at the open carton of cookbooks Ivan set on the floor. "Of course, if you run out I've brought my own supply."

Ivan looked at her as if she'd stepped off another planet. Among his rumored talents was a stint at Le Cordon Bleu in Paris and some high-end restaurant experience in a few major cities. He might appear to be a simple guy in bookseller mode but there was a lot the average person never knew about him. Surely he knew of Farrel O'Hearn's reputation and would carry her book if it was likely to sell locally.

Sam gave him a surreptitious wink and turned away, trying to remember what she'd been about to do before the distraction.

Raised voices near the doors to the corridor caught her attention. Carinda Carter stood just inside the ballroom, staring at the dais. She'd apparently just made some comment to Rupert because he stood with a pair of large shears in hand and Sam swore that he subtly shifted them so they would make an easy weapon. She hurried over.

"Rupert? What's—?"

"I thought *I* was to decorate the dais," Carinda shouted.

Sam glanced at Rupert, whose eyes begged her not to suggest that they do it together. Sam straightened her shoulders.

"Nope, Carinda. That's Rupert's job. I had you on the list for . . ." she thought frantically "uh . . . for coordinating vendor services." She had no idea what that meant but had to come up with some sort of title. "For their comfort, we want to be sure each vendor has bottled water and, if they wish, sodas or coffee. If you can go around and ask each of them what they would like, and then see that Mr. Handler gets a list, that would be a huge help. Once everyone is set up, probably later this afternoon, we have goodie bags to hand out and I would love it if you could take on that responsibility."

Rupert, having taken over nearly everything to do with their Swiss sponsor, looked a little miffed but once Carinda set out to take drink orders Sam pacified him with the reminder that at least now she wasn't right in his face. He grumbled a little but soon became distracted again as he and Kelly hung bunting across the front of the judges' table. Sam remembered that she'd been about to call Sweet's Sweets so she stepped out to the corridor where it was marginally quieter.

Near the garden door there was a steady stream of foot traffic, people whose arms were laden with boxes as they came indoors, empty as they went back for more. She edged closer to the less-crowded lobby, ducking aside as Harvey rushed past as if he didn't see her standing there.

"Julio has everything loaded into the van," Becky told Sam. "He can break away from here as soon as his cinnamon rolls come out of the oven."

"Perfect." Sam remembered that she and Beau had tentatively talked about getting together for lunch, but there was no way she was getting out of here now.

She gave him a quick call, declining his generous offer to bring her a sandwich. She'd barely had time to make the phone call—when would she manage a chance to eat?

"I hope to be out of here close to six o'clock," she said. "All vendors were instructed to have their setup done by then."

"Good luck with that," he said with a little chuckle. "When does everyone in a group of people actually follow what they're told?"

She let out a sigh; he was so right.

She wandered back into the ballroom, spotting Harvey Byron's portable freezer bin with the striped awning above and logo for his shop, Ice Cream Social. A woman with long blonde hair stood near it, her back toward Sam at the moment. She apparently spotted Carinda across the room because she called out her name and headed toward the east end of the room, but when Sam scanned the crowd, Carinda had vanished again.

Just as well. Sam really hoped to avoid the prickly woman for the rest of the day, if possible. Sweet's Sweets was right next to Harvey's Ice Cream Social booth and she headed that direction. On the other side of her spot, a woman stood in the open space looking a little lost.

"I'm Nancy Nash," the woman said after Sam introduced herself. "I didn't realize we had to bring everything. Everyone else has such nice decorations and stuff."

"Well, you don't have to go fancy with it, but it was

explained in the instruction sheet we sent out when your application was approved. I'm sorry, I don't remember what your product is."

"Oh, well, I don't have a shop or anything. I decided to enter my famous chocolate-covered strawberries."

"Ooh, that sounds really good."

"Well, my family loves them. I never tell the kids how really easy they are to make." Nancy raised both hands to her temples, pressing with her fingertips and squeezing her eyes shut. "Ow."

"Are you okay?"

"The hum. It's so *loud* right now." She opened one eye. "You don't hear it?"

The Taos Hum. Sam had heard *of* it for years—she'd never actually heard the sound itself. Despite the efforts of scientists to capture it, no definitive proof had surfaced to their satisfaction. Meanwhile, those who claimed to hear the sound described it, variously, as a swarm of bees, a low diesel engine or a faraway locomotive. At the moment, all Sam could hear was the clamor of voices in the crowded room.

She gave a rueful smile and shook her head. "I guess I'm not one of the sensitive ones."

"It can be anything from annoying to excruciating. Sometimes I feel like I'm going crazy, like I want to hit something," Nancy said, lowering her hands. "There, it's fading now."

Sam's phone rang before she was forced to comment. Julio had arrived in the unloading zone and needed help to get the van cleared in his allocated fifteen minutes. Sam hurried away to round up Kelly and Rupert and they rushed out through the garden.

When they arrived back at the booth with their first load—two tables carried by Rupert and a Plexiglas display case, which Sam and Kelly managed between them—Nancy Nash gave their setup a critical eye, said "oh, my" and left.

"Apparently she thought the organizers provide everything or that somehow tables and booths can magically grow out of the floor," Sam said to Kelly.

"Or, like nearly everyone, she just didn't read the instructions."

Julio arrived with a second display case. Sam had found the covered displays at a wholesale place. They weren't nearly as nice as the antiques with curved glass in the shop, but she'd found them attractive enough for the times when she might sell her baked goods from another location. As if she would *ever* want to go through this again.

By the time she and Rupert had unfolded the table legs and righted them, Kelly came back with a box containing cloth table skirts in the shop's signature purple tones. She quickly draped both tables, positioned them and the two women set the display cases in place. Rupert and Julio each carried in another carton—it seemed to require a hundred items, from pens to credit card processing machine to bags and tissue paper for handling the food.

"I better move the van, Sam," Julio said. "Call us if we've forgotten anything."

"That's the most I've ever heard him say," Kelly whispered after Julio walked away.

"He's a man of few words, for sure. But he makes up for it with his knowledge in the kitchen."

"I better get back to the dais," Rupert said. "I'm trying to come up with chairs for the judges, something more comfortable than the standard-issue metal ones the hotel brought first." He hurried away.

"And, I'll bet he doesn't want anyone getting into the chocolate samples," Kelly said. "I sneaked one—they are amazing."

"Speaking of chairs . . ." Sam jotted a note. "I hadn't even thought of it, but there might be lulls when a chance to sit down will feel really good. We'll bring a couple of the bistro chairs from the shop tomorrow."

Her thoughts were interrupted by a female shriek. Sam stared around the area; the sounds of an argument rose from the far end of the room, near the kitchen door.

What now? she thought, hurrying toward what was quickly becoming a full-blown fight.

"—on the same aisle as *her*!" The speaker stood facing Carinda Carter with her arms folded tightly beneath an ample chest, her blue eyes flashing and blond hair standing up in spikes that may have been even more rigid than originally intended.

"Ms. Ferguson, please calm down. We can sort this out." Carinda sounded, for once, like the voice of reason.

Sam recognized the chef from Chatsworth's, a local restaurant that prided itself on high-end desserts that sold for as much as the entrees.

"Danielle, hi. What's the problem?"

"Farrel O'Hearn. She's *always* a problem. Had I known she would be here, well, I would have suggested to Chatsworth that we skip the whole tawdry event."

"What's the matter? Can't handle the competition?"

Sam spun around to find that Farrel O'Hearn had walked up behind her.

"Ladies—keep it civil, all right?"

"I'm sure whatever Chatsworth Bingham has you cooking up, it won't bring too much shame on this *tawdry* event. There's no way it will beat my entry. I can promise you that."

"Ladies—watch your words. We're doing this festival for charity. Please keep that in mind." Sam started to order Farrel back to her own booth but the redhead had turned away.

"Witch! I intend to win this thing—at all cost—and she'd better get used to the idea. Who assigned me this spot anyway?" Danielle demanded.

Carinda shot a triumphant look toward Sam. "*She* insisted on doing the booth assignments."

As if Carinda herself would have known that these two women were arch rivals.

"Carinda . . . don't you have some other duties at the moment?"

This time the look was a glare. Carinda muttered something about why was she bothering to put up with this bunch and stomped across the ballroom where she apparently thought she had an ally in one of the vendors whom she had admitted to the festival at the last minute.

Sam stared after her for a moment. Again, the reference to not being here long. With any luck, Carinda was one of those summer people who came for a few months and would leave Taos behind in the fall. Heaven forbid that she become a regular volunteer at every event in town. The rest of the populace would be ready to move away if they had to deal with her much longer.

Danielle Ferguson seemed to be waiting for an answer to her question.

"Where in the room would you like to be?" Sam asked, scanning the space for possibilities. Nearly all the other vendors were already here and at least partially set up. Moving one of them would not go over well. "My booth is over there, the one with the Sweet's Sweets sign. I'll switch with you if it makes a difference."

Danielle's eyes widened. "You're practically right across the aisle from *her*—no way!"

"We'll refund your fee if you want to withdraw—there's a waiting list for spaces. Otherwise, I expect peace and quiet from everyone. You and Farrel are more than five booths apart, but you have to make nice."

Danielle considered for a minute. Clearly, her boss at the restaurant would not be happy if his was the only high-class establishment in town not represented. She grumbled a bit but went back to the task of setting up her display. Sam turned toward Farrel's end of the aisle. The redhead was laughing a bit too heartily at something Rupert must have said, showing off for Danielle that she wasn't bothered in the least.

"Excuse me? Do you know where I might find Carinda Carter?" The tall, blonde woman looked somewhat familiar but she had spoken to Danielle so Sam started to walk away.

"Whoever that is," said Danielle. "Sam?"

"She was just here a minute ago. Now she's right over—" Sam started to point across the room but she didn't see Carinda anywhere. "Hm. Well, she has to be around."

The woman headed toward the row of booths by the windows, while Sam stewed. Most of the Sweet Somethings banners still needed to be hung, along with setting up the ticket table and making sure the pamphlets and ballots were in the right places. Why was it that when the real work began Carinda always seemed to dash out to do something more important?

Chapter 9

By six o'clock Sam felt dead on her feet. She never had caught up with Carinda Carter so she, Kelly and Rupert had hung all the banners and completed the final preparations. Danielle Ferguson was the last of the vendors to leave, still carping about the fact that Farrel O'Hearn was allowed in the competition—she wasn't local, after all. Sam had the distinct feeling this all went to some desperate need on Danielle's part to win the top prize. The blonde had as much as said so. Frankly, she was sick of the whole bunch of them and glad that she wouldn't have an entry in the contest.

Beau was on his way out the door when she arrived at home.

"Hey you." He pulled her close. "You look like a girl who doesn't want to cook dinner."

She nodded against his chest, her cheek scraping on his badge.

"If you want to ride along with me while I have a little talk with the hippie dude I'll take you out for the dinner of your choice afterward."

A shower would have felt good but not having to stress over the meal felt better. She followed him to his department cruiser. The ride out to the highway, taking the next turn and pulling in at the Mulvane property took all of four minutes, just long enough for Sam to begin feeling drowsy in the passenger seat.

Beau parked next to one of the blue buses, the one that had been there from the beginning.

"Want to come with me or wait here?" he asked.

She looked toward the bus and saw three kids with ratty yellow hair staring at her from the windows. No way would she fall asleep under their careful scrutiny.

"I'll go along." She unclipped her seatbelt and got out, watching as Beau asked at the bus door for someone named Moondoggie.

Seriously? Those nicknames hadn't faded away after the sixties?

The braless woman whose hair was identical to her kids' pointed toward an open spot where a bunch of white-painted stones formed a circle about thirty feet in diameter. "He's in the middle," she said.

Moondoggie had a neatly trimmed beard and a fringe of dark hair surrounding a shiny bald pate. Without the white tunic, loose white pants and sandals he could have put on a business suit and fit in at nearly any corporate office in the country. Sam wondered if perhaps he did just that after his summer sojourn each year.

He watched as they approached, hands clasped together at his waist. When Beau said hello, Moondoggie pressed his palms together and gave a little bow.

"Greetings. Welcome to the Summer of Peace encampment." His soft voice had a smooth quality that really did convey a tone of tranquility.

Beau nodded. "I'm touching base because Mr. Mulvane is concerned over the number of vehicles on his land. He says there are a lot more people in your group than he was led to believe."

"The movement is an ever-changing thing. Those who follow our vision of peace upon the entire planet are a growing segment of the population. We welcome any and all who seek to live in accord with their fellow beings."

Beau looked around. "Yeah, I get that. How long do you plan to stay?"

"The arrival of Midsommar—what you might call the summer solstice—portends many great earthly and heavenly events this year. Our gathering will focus on the auspicious confluence of the solstice, a lunar eclipse, and the juxtaposition of Scorpio and Taurus in the heavens. We intend to bring together the amazing energy of the universe with the global desire for harmony. With that sort of movement, we believe we can achieve world peace, if only during the moments of the eclipse."

Beau's right eyebrow went up. Sam had no idea whether Moondoggie knew what he was talking about but calculated that the answer to Beau's question was that the group intended to stay at least a couple more weeks.

Beau took a different tack. "There's a lot of trash blowing around on the ground and I don't see any toilets. Plus, you do realize that your group is subject to the same fire restrictions that are in effect throughout the state and county? You've got to keep your campfires contained within dirt or stone pits and allow a minimum thirty feet of bare earth around each one."

"Quite so. We want only the best for our Mother Earth." Moondoggie's beneficent expression took on a harder edge, just a touch. "We do have a contractual right to be here upon this place. Mr. Mulvane was quite agreeable."

"He says he has not received the balance of payment that the contract calls for. Based on that fact, you would be in breach of contract and he can ask that you vacate."

Moondoggie reached into a deep pocket within the folds of his loose pants and pulled out a wad of cash.

"The payment will be made this evening. We are completely legal."

"I'm sure the landowner will appreciate that. Meanwhile, just be aware that my department will check back now and then, making sure the trash is contained and the sanitation situation has been addressed properly."

"Properly . . ." Moondoggie's gaze drifted skyward, a silent prayer for the obtuseness of the law, most likely.

Beau scanned the encampment. Nothing seemed to pose a threat at the moment so there wasn't much else he could do. He reminded the hippie leader to be sure he paid Mulvane the money they owed, then he and Sam walked back to the cruiser.

"I hope the next three weeks go uneventfully," Sam said as Beau pulled onto the highway.

"I didn't get the impression they were necessarily leaving right after their big peace rally. They could end up staying the whole summer. Mulvane was a fool for not specifying a termination date to that contract. He's basically given them access for as long as they want to stay."

"Well, that makes my current headaches seem like nothing at all. At least this festival will be done and gone in three more days. End of story, and I won't volunteer for another one, that's for sure."

Beau pointed toward their favorite pizza place, just ahead, and when Sam nodded he turned in. They took a table by the windows and ordered what seemed like the lightest thing on the menu.

"Don't let me eat much tonight. I have a feeling I'll be sampling chocolate *everything* for the next few days. You should at least come by and try some things, Beau. Each vendor will choose his or her best item and submit it anonymously to the judging panel. We've got a couple of prominent locals and one actual celebrity from Hollywood."

"It almost sounds like fun," he admitted, "but you've already told me too much about the battles between those women on your committee. Hyped up on chocolate . . . I can only imagine the carnage. I'd better stick with my usual, and hope that I don't have anything much more serious than some speeding tickets to hand out."

They finished their pizza and went home for an early bedtime. Although the doors for the festival wouldn't open until ten the next morning, Sam knew there were still a hundred details to attend to. She set her alarm for her usual four-thirty.

* * *

Becky and Jen, both looking a little haggard at this extra-early hour, met her at Sweet's Sweets at six o'clock. They would help her load the van and stock their booth, then Jen would return to make sales all day in the shop. Becky and Sam could run the booth and, with luck, take custom orders and add a lot of new customers to their regular clientele.

Sam had made two ambitious creations for display: a bathtub-shaped cake, complete with claw feet and gold trim, spilling over with edible gelatin 'bubbles' in pale pink and a traditional wedding cake covered in sleek, pale-lavender fondant with trim of rose-gold beading and delicate miniature garden flowers in all shades of purple. She had to admit that they were two of her finest examples. If someone wanted to buy either of them, she would insist they pick them up at the end of the event. A flashy 'Sold' sign would surely instill urgency in the minds of other customers.

"I think I pretty well sorted the festival goodies from what we normally need in the shop," Becky said. "The top two shelves in the fridge are what we need to load into the van."

"Check everything, though, just to be sure," Sam suggested as she stepped into the big walk-in. "It would be a mess if we sold slices of someone's birthday cake."

They worked quickly to fill the van before the day began to warm up. Jen followed in her car as Sam led the way to the hotel. Already, two other vehicles were in the loading zone. Harvey Byron apologized for taking extra space but his ice cream was even more fragile than Sam's frostings. At least the others were moving as quickly as possible and soon it was Sam's turn.

The sun began to fully hit the parking lot as they were wheeling the last stack of boxes through the garden and into the corridor by the ballroom.

"I'll move your van over by those trees," Jen said, "then

I'm on my way back to open the shop. Good luck—or is that break-a-leg or something?"

Sam laughed. "Let's hope nothing gets broken. Call me if you need anything, although I'm sure you and Julio can handle it fine."

"It'll probably be slow. I think everyone in town will be over here."

"We sold more than a thousand advance tickets, and people can still get theirs at the door." Even as she said it, Sam began to feel a little overwhelmed.

Carinda Carter rushed toward her before Sam had gotten to the ballroom door.

"Bentley Day arrived last night! I offered to act as his assistant." She was practically quivering with this news.

Sam noticed that she was wearing a blue dress that fit her slender body very well and her hair was freshly styled. How Carinda looked really didn't matter, Sam decided; at least she seemed in a decent mood at the moment.

"I've checked in with our celebrity already this morning," Carinda said, "to be sure he had a good night's sleep."

Poor guy.

"I suggested that he come down soon to meet all the contestants, but he seemed a little out of sorts and wanted more time over his coffee."

Sam couldn't imagine anyone *not* being out of sorts if the first voice they heard in the early morning was Carinda's. She merely nodded and headed into the ballroom.

"I got the impression he wants to primp a little and then make a grand entrance," Carinda was saying, trotting along beside Sam. "But I did offer to bring his props downstairs ahead of time. See? Even his famous chef's knife."

She tugged at Sam's sleeve and directed her attention to a box beneath the skirted table at the judging stand. A white cloth chef's hat lay atop several other items—who knew what little egocentric things a reality TV star would carry with him? Probably photos he could hand out to fans and cards with his phone number for the extra pretty ones. While Carinda was absorbed in her own importance as Bentley Day's assistant, Sam walked toward her own booth to help Becky finish setting out their products.

"Only a hour before the doors open to the crowds," Becky said, shifting a tray of brownies forward in the display case to make room for the boxed chocolate pueblos. "Do you really think people will be gobbling down all this chocolate at ten in the morning?"

"Well, we sell a lot of it to the midmorning coffee crowd at the shop."

"Coffee! We should have brought—"

"I think Java Joe has that covered," Sam said. She had actually thought of bringing carafes of her signature blend, but the local coffee shop had a huge following so why not let him do all the work?

Voices rose near Farrel O'Hearn's booth and Sam glanced up to see Danielle Ferguson standing there. Farrel had her back to Sam but the tension in her shoulders was evident and the way her head bobbed as she spoke emphasized that the words must be emotional. *If I have to step in and separate you two again* . . . Sam gritted her teeth.

In the booth next to Sam's, Nancy Nash glanced up briefly but went back to pouring ice cream syrup from a bottle into a small crockery cooker. Sam felt her eyes go wide. Was this the super-special recipe Nancy's family loved so much—strawberries dipped in plain bottled syrup?

Nancy caught her looking and turned away to stash the bottle out of sight.

Danielle had moved on, her spiky blonde hair bobbing as she walked toward her own booth.

"Okay, I have officially had it with that woman," Rupert said, startling Sam as he edged in close, approaching from the opposite direction from where she'd been looking.

"Danielle or Farrel?"

"Carinda! She's out there in the corridor ordering the two volunteer ladies around. All they have to do is take tickets and Carinda is acting as if she's the only person in the world who could handle it."

"So, let her. Let her handle everything and see how quickly she cries for help," Becky offered.

Sam piped up. "You know what—she's not worth it. Don't let yourself get in a twist, Rupert."

"All I can say is that she better stay out of my way. I've offered to MC this thing but I don't have to take orders from Miss Skinny Britches over there."

As if she'd been summoned, Carinda came through the wide doorway and headed straight for Sam's booth. Rupert scooted past Nancy's spot and kept on going. Sam saw him make a wide circle of the room and go into the corridor at the east end near the kitchen.

"The mandatory vendor meeting is supposed to start in fifteen minutes," Carinda stated abruptly. "I think it would be a good idea if Bentley Day were present—you know, to meet the contestants, give everyone a little cheerio, good wishes and all."

Mandatory meeting? Sam glanced at the printed schedule, which had fallen to the floor under her table. It did say that all vendors should be set up no later than nine forty-five;

how did that turn into a mandatory meeting?

"So anyway, I'll run upstairs, give Bentley a little nudge and bring him down." Carinda was off before Sam could say anything.

"I swear, she's the most irritating person," Becky said under her voice. Strong words, coming from the usually mellow Becky. "I'm still trying to figure out why she thinks she has to report every little thing to you, and yet she goes ahead and acts on her own anyway."

Good question. Sam took a deep breath. A glance around the room showed that Danielle Ferguson had not returned to her booth yet and Farrel O'Hearn was also out of sight, hopefully not tracking Danielle and making that situation even worse. It was going to be a very long weekend.

She turned her attention to finishing the Sweet's Sweets display, arranging rows of cookies and slices of cheesecake. The girls had insisted she include her secret recipe amaretto cheesecake, even though it contained no chocolate—her regular customers would expect to see it and she couldn't afford to pass up that many word-of-mouth recommendations. They placed the two showpieces—the bathtub cake and the purple-themed wedding cake—on pedestals at each end of the booth, then Sam stepped out to the aisle to give their display a final perusal.

"Looks good," she said, checking the time.

They should do a few announcements and introduce the judges before the doors opened. Already she could hear the low buzz created by a sizeable crowd coming from the hotel lobby and the end of the corridor the other side of their ticket table. Where was Bentley Day? Carinda had gone to get him more than twenty minutes ago.

She scanned the room but didn't spot either of them. All

the vendors were in their booths, making a few final touches or just relaxing with coffee before the bombardment. Check that—Farrel O'Hearn's assistant was alone in her booth. Danielle was back now and by the look on her face, the two of them may have had another altercation; the buxom blonde seemed agitated, with two spots of color on her cheeks that were visible even across the length of the large room.

Sam walked to the double doors opening into the hall and peered out. The two young ticket takers were chatting nervously at the sight of the crowd but there was no sign of Carinda or Bentley.

Back at the dais, the other two judges—the mayor's wife and police chief's wife—were in their seats, looking a little unsure about what they should be doing. Rupert bustled past them and walked up to Sam.

"We better take over this thing," he whispered. "You start with whatever information you want the vendors to know. Then I'll introduce the judges. If Mr. Day isn't here by then . . . well, everyone knows who he is anyway."

Sam went with him and picked up the microphone. A few words about sticking to the schedule, and about preparing their contest entries.

"Someone from the committee will come around to pick up your entry. Use the generic white plate that was provided in your packets and be sure to include the little numbered tag also. All entries are anonymous, so it's a fair contest for everyone. There are nice prizes on the line and we want to be sure every aspect of the judging is done fairly."

She handed over the mike to Rupert who introduced the two lady judges and announced that Bentley Day would be joining them shortly.

"And now, Mrs. Mayor, would you please officially open the festival?"

The dark-haired woman beamed, clearly comfortable with speaking to a crowd as her beautiful smile and stylish clothing had been a big reason for her husband's election to the town's top office after a series of political rallies last fall. She welcomed everyone, made a joke about how much weight she would probably gain this weekend, and ended with, "Let the chocolate begin!"

Rupert must have signaled the ticket girls because the wide doorways were suddenly filled with people. They flowed like a molten stream into the room, branching out to the booths with exclamations over each new discovery. From the height of the dais Rupert glanced toward Sam's booth and gave her an exaggerated wink.

Two women who were regulars in Sam's shop immediately recognized her sign and came straight to the booth.

"I just couldn't wait to see what special thing you've made this time," said Mrs. Greenbaum, her white fluffy head bobbing as she scrutinized the items in the display. "Oh! I bet it's those little candies shaped like the pueblo."

"You are right—they're exclusive to the festival," Becky said.

"Have one, on the house." Sam picked up one of the chocolates with tongs and held it out. Of course, Mrs. Riley had to have one too.

"That is fabulous—I'll take a dozen of them." Mrs. Greenbaum reached into her purse. "Do you have change for a fifty?"

Becky's face went pale. "I knew there was something I

forgot to bring inside. The cash bag you brought from the shop—it's still in the van. I'll run get it."

Sam sent a smile toward the two ladies. "There's always some little forgotten detail, isn't there?"

They assured her it was fine; while Becky rushed out they continued to browse the display, pointing out molten lava cupcakes, s'mores brownies and chocolate nut drop cookies, each filling a bag.

Sam found herself glancing toward the doors. Becky's errand seemed to be taking a long time. When she spotted her assistant, Becky was rushing along the crowded aisle. Something was definitely wrong. Pushing her way into the booth, she handed the money bag over to Sam and turned her back on the customers.

Sam quickly made change for the two women, excused herself a moment to the others who were browsing, and turned to get a good look at Becky. The younger woman's face was pale and her hands shook.

"What happened out there?"

Becky glanced toward the throngs of people in the room. Her voice came out a ragged whisper.

"There's a—a body, out in the garden. I'm pretty sure she's dead."

Sam felt the blood drain from her face. Of all the disasters that might have happened at the festival, this was one she'd never considered. "I wonder who—?"

"It's Carinda Carter."

Chapter 10

Sam took Becky's shoulders and forced her to stand still. "Did you call the police?"

Becky shook her head.

"We need to do that. I'll find someplace private—" A distant scream interrupted.

Sam turned to the customers in front of her booth. "I'll be right back. Just let Becky know what you want."

She shot Becky a look that said, *take your mind off the other and just stay busy.* Edging out of the booth, she met the challenge of speed walking and looking nonchalant at the same time. The single scream had largely been ignored inside the ballroom. Once Sam was past the corridor she rushed to the garden.

A hotel maid had dropped a stack of white towels onto the damp lawn; she stood with both hands to her mouth, her eyes wide. Sam reached her at the same time as a gardener. On the ground, among the rose bushes, lay Carinda Carter in her tight blue dress. Unfortunately, the shiny fabric was marred by a massive red stain spreading from the hilt of a large knife that protruded from her back. By the angle of her limbs, she was most assuredly dead.

"Has anyone called the authorities?" Sam asked.

The maid seemed in danger of hyperventilating. Sam gestured to the gardener to lead her away from the body, while she pulled out her phone.

The hotel was outside the town limits so this would fall in Beau's jurisdiction. She felt as if her explanation probably came out garbled, but he got it. He said he and his men would be right there.

Time stood still but it couldn't have been more than five minutes before she heard sirens. Damn. She met the first cruiser at the curb in the loading zone, recognized Rico, one of Beau's deputies, and rushed toward him, explaining that a festival was going on inside and if they didn't want several hundred people to come rushing out into the crime scene, it would be better to do this quietly. He got on the radio and when two more cars arrived, it was without fanfare.

Sam pointed Rico in the direction of the rose garden, although one of the other men stayed behind and started to ask questions. Who had discovered the body? Did she know the deceased? Where had she been when she heard the maid scream? She was becoming impatient with the quizzing and worried about going back to her booth when Beau drove up.

He sent the deputy to mark off the crime scene.

"I need to get back to Becky and make sure she's okay," she said. "I think it would be best if questions about the murder were done away from the crowd inside. Of the hundreds of people here in the hotel, only a handful really even knew this woman. I can give you a list."

Beau walked with her as they circled the ribbon of yellow crime scene tape. One of the deputies was already snapping photos and collecting evidence around the body. "Don't let people inside start talking about this. Just advise everyone to cooperate when it's their turn to answer questions, but remember that anyone has the right to an attorney if they want one."

She nodded, a little impatiently. Who on earth didn't already know this?

"I'll get Kelly to take over my booth so Becky can talk to you. *And* I'll pass along your words of wisdom." She started to open the heavy door to the corridor but turned back to him. "Oh, Beau, who would do this? I mean, Carinda was really irritating, but who would hate her this much?"

He pulled her into a hug and rubbed her back as he murmured soothing sounds. "We'll talk later, once I get this organized."

"Thanks. I'll be in my booth near the northwest corner of the ballroom."

Becky looked a little better when Sam arrived. Bagging cookies and boxing up slices of cheesecake for customers had helped bring the color back to her face, although her hands were still pretty shaky.

"What's going on out there?" she whispered to Sam when a slight lull came in the activity around the booth.

"A lot of standard procedure, I suppose. Beau or one of his deputies will want to talk to both of us. Don't worry. You just tell them what you saw. I'll go find Kelly now. She'll help out here while we're busy with that."

She headed toward the dais, where she'd last seen Rupert chatting with the police chief's sister just before Sam had returned to her booth. The woman was tapping something into her cell phone and Rupert's princely head of hair showed above the gathering out in the corridor. Sam breezed past the dais and caught up with her friend.

"Dish, girl. What's going on around here?" he asked when she tapped his arm.

"I need to find Kelly. Have you seen her?"

"Over by the ticket table." He gripped her wrist. "Wait-wait-wait. What's the deal?"

Sam took a breath and pulled him into a small alcove away from the traffic. "Carinda's been killed. Beau's men are here and I'm doing my best to keep it as quiet as possible. Do *not* say anything to *anyone*. They'll want to talk to everybody who saw or spoke with her in the last few hours."

Rupert actually blanched.

"Rupe? Did you have another run-in with her?"

He waved away the thought. "I just had a brilliant idea for a scene in my next book."

Writers. Sheesh. Sam reminded him to keep quiet before she hustled off to catch up with Kelly.

"I'll need you to handle my booth for awhile."

"Sure, Mom." Kelly gave Sam a hard stare. "What's going on around here? It's like there's an electric current running through the carpeting."

She might as well make an announcement over the PA. But that would lead to complete chaos.

"Tell you later. Whatever is said, please just brush it off and keep selling brownies, okay?"

A man in jeans and a leather jacket was standing at the booth when Sam and Kelly approached, and Becky seemed shaken all over again. It was one of Beau's deputies—Ben Garcia.

"Hi, Sam. Beau asked me to take preliminary statements. Not being in uniform, I guess, will make people less nervous with me."

Sam assured Becky it was all right to go with him. Luckily, a large group of customers walked up just then so Sam and Kelly had no opportunity to talk about anything but baked goods for the next fifteen minutes. Becky returned, looking more relaxed than she had since the discovery, and told Sam that Ben Garcia was ready to talk to her now. She gave directions to a room on the second floor. Sam sent a warning glare toward both of the younger women. *Do not talk about this here!*

Garcia smiled and offered coffee when she entered the room, which Auguste Handler must have offered as a temporary interrogation space. It looked like the living room portion of a small suite. She gratefully accepted the coffee and sat on the couch he indicated. He flipped through a little notebook before asking what she knew of Carinda's movements that morning.

"Last I saw of her she said she was going to rouse our celebrity judge and get him downstairs before the doors opened to the public. Now that I think of it I haven't seen him, even yet."

"Did you or your committee people have any problems or arguments with Ms. Carter?" Garcia asked. "Beau kind of hinted."

Let me count the ways . . . "Carinda has—had—a way about her. She managed to antagonize people just by walking into a room. Of our committee—" She stopped. What was she doing? Handing her friends over for something that surely none of them would have done? "Let's just say that she was pushy and irritating, but everyone knew to blow it off and stay out of her way."

"Were there specific incidents that provoked anger? Stabbing someone involves a lot of rage—anyone dislike her that much?"

Sam recounted what she could remember—the woman's uncanny ability to butt into every aspect of the festival planning but when the real work began how she could manage to vanish. "But I never saw anyone actually threaten her. Truly, her mannerisms were more of an annoyance."

"We'll need to locate her next of kin. Do you know who that might be?"

Sam shook her head. "She never talked about family. I got the idea that she was really new in town and had joined our committee because she had no one else to be close to."

He nodded and jotted more notes. Sam got the impression he was finished with the questions.

"Oh," he said, reaching beside his chair and picking up a sealed evidence bag. "Do you recognize this?"

The bag contained a large and deadly looking knife, complete with blood. Sam's stomach lurched. It looked like Bentley Day's famous chef knife from his TV show. On the handle, a metal medallion had the show's logo. She'd assumed it was only a prop, not actually sharp enough to inflict damage.

"Carinda showed me this knife, just this morning. It was in a box of items belonging to Bentley Day."

"Bentley Day . . ." he scribbled as he said the name. "Is that *the* Bentley Day from *Killer Chef*?"

"I—I—yes, it is." Sam's thoughts tumbled in her head like bingo numbers in a hopper. "This doesn't look too good for him, does it?"

"He would have had to come down to the ballroom to retrieve the knife before meeting Ms. Carter in the garden. Surely someone would have noticed a celebrity among the crowd?"

True. And no one had mentioned seeing him this morning. So, what did that mean?

Garcia didn't seem to expect an answer. He stood up and Sam followed suit, glad to leave the room but a little shaken that she'd come away with far more questions than answers. Bentley Day's prints would surely be on the knife, but then so would Carinda's and probably half the people she'd been showing it to. On the way back down to the ballroom Sam wondered whether any of her inner circle of friends would be among them. She really wished she could sneak Beau away from the garden right now and discuss all this.

In the downstairs corridor, Sam caught a flash of white heading into the ballroom. She followed, just in time to catch a murmur passing through the crowd.

"G'day, Taos!" The man in kitchen whites standing on the dais with both arms raised must be Bentley Day. Curly blond hair in some kind of a shaggy cut peeked out below the band of the chef's hat on his head. He ramped up the volume on the Aussie accent: "I say, g'day, Taos!"

A cheer rocked the room and people crammed as close to the judging table as they could get. Both of the female judges had retreated to the back of the space on the platform.

"What do you say, we eat some great chocolate!"

Crowd roar.

"What do we do in the kitchen?" Apparently some kind of *Killer Chef* buzzword.

"Chop! Chop!" the crowd roared.

"Yeah, chop-chop!" Day picked up a large knife from the table and swished it through the air twice.

Sam flinched. How did he get that thing back—? Then she realized he surely owned more than one of them.

"Where's my cake?!" he shouted.

Someone set a paper plate with a small chocolate cake in front of him. He whacked it with the knife and crumbs flew. The crowd went wild.

"Chop-chop!" they shouted.

He chopped a few more times until there was nothing left of the poor cake. Sam caught Rupert's eye. This was in incredibly poor taste, considering the morning's tragedy. She tilted her head toward the door and he edged out into the hall with her.

"Thank goodness almost no one here knows that a woman was stabbed this morning," she whispered. "This little show takes on almost obscene proportions in light of that."

Rupert, for once in his life, seemed a little at a loss. "It's the standard introduction he uses at the beginning of every show. He'll settle down in a minute."

"He'd better. Maybe this is a good time for you to step in and take over as MC?"

He nodded, crossed the corridor and pushed back into the crowded ballroom. Sam watched as Rupert nearly leapt up the steps to the dais and picked up the microphone.

"Thank you, Bentley Day! How about this guy, folks? Is he as crazy as on TV, huh?"

Okay, Rupe, tune all of it down a notch, Sam thought. She walked to the other set of doors, the less crowded end near the kitchen, and stepped into the ballroom. Deputy Garcia stood there, watching the celebrity's antics with a grim expression. Uh-oh.

"Looks like there was more than one knife," she said when he noticed her.

"That does add another wrinkle to it." His eyes were scanning the booths, watching each of the vendors, most of whom were riveted to the scene at the head of the room.

Rupert had edged his co-star away from center stage as he proceeded to give the rules for the contest.

"As you know, the Swiss chocolate maker *Qualitätsschokolade* has offered cash prizes for the best desserts made with their products, and we have three esteemed judges here to do the tasting and make the call. All of our contestants have booths here today, so you can taste the scrumptious entries yourselves. Be sure to use the form on the back of your ticket to nominate your favorite for the People's Choice Award. There is a separate prize for this one, and you will make someone's day if his or her name is chosen.

"All contestants will submit a sample of their best recipe today. The top ten will go into a semi-final round. Tomorrow, those entries will be narrowed to five, and on Sunday the top three will be awarded prizes. Third place wins two thousand dollars cash!"

Applause throughout the room.

"Second place will receive three thousand dollars."

Another wave of appreciation.

"And the first place entry gets five thousand dollars—"

This time the cheers caused him to pause.

"—plus the winning baker will get an appearance on *Killer Chef!*"

The room rocked with cheers and shouts. Sam wondered if Rupert had made that up on the spot, hoping to sell the producers on the idea, or if Bentley Day had made the offer before coming up on stage. Whatever the situation, she had to admit that stretching out the judging over several days *and* the award of the high-profile prize would definitely be good for the charity for which all this fundraising was happening.

"Contestants ready?" Rupert threw every bit of his enthusiasm into the call. "Get set . . . Here come the judging assistants to pick up your entries!"

To keep the judging impartial, each baker would place three small servings of his or her entry on a plain white paper plate, along with a number which did not correspond to the booth from which it came. The plate was covered with a napkin until it reached the judging table, theoretically preventing anyone in the crowd from knowing and whispering ideas to the judges. It wouldn't take a rocket scientist to circumvent the system, but at least the efforts attempted to give equal footing to all.

Sam circled to her booth, relieving Kelly who was one of the entry-delivery helpers. While the visitors were enthralled with watching judge reactions to the first few desserts, Sam found herself watching the vendors. Garcia was quietly making his way around the room, speaking in low tones and taking names and contact information from them. At Danielle Ferguson's booth, he asked her to step outside. Luckily, she had an assistant to take over sales of her elegant tortes.

Sam wondered what was going on. By now, surely they had removed Carinda's body. The hotel would certainly want the crime scene tape gone as soon as possible; this could not be good for business. Auguste Handler's job had just become harder, dealing with the PR nightmare associated with having a murder on the property.

"You're distracted, Sam." Becky was staring at her. "Go. Do whatever it is you're wanting to. There's a lull right now—I can handle the booth."

What she really wanted to do was talk to Beau. After Becky assured her once again that she would be fine alone, Sam walked out of the ballroom. She stepped out the back door to the garden, didn't see him among the men who were still gathering evidence, so she went toward the lobby.

Through the large windows across the front of the hotel she saw a different sort of crowd. The medical investigator's vehicle disappeared around a bend in the long driveway, and now Beau had a half-dozen microphones shoved toward him. Looked as if the press invited to cover the chocolate festival had now latched onto the crime instead.

Chapter 11

Sam's white baker's jacket drew looks from a few of the reporters but they quickly realized she was nobody they might be interested in.

"Sheriff, is it true that Bentley Day is your main suspect?"

Beau seemed a little startled. "Where did you hear that?"

The questioner held up her cell phone, on which the Twitter logo was easily recognizable. "It's all over the place."

Sam had sidled toward the group; now she saw messages on several phones. Bentley Day being quizzed by cops showed on one. Is Killer Chef really a killer? blazed across another, with responding messages coming through fast and furiously.

Where had this started? Sam felt her temper rise. Carinda might have been a pain in the ass and Bentley Day grandstanding and full of himself, but it didn't necessarily follow that he killed her. Aside from wishing he could swat her like an annoying mosquito, what motive would he have?

Beau answered nearly every question with something along the lines of "It's too early in the investigation to make any assumptions" and "We're in the process of gathering evidence and asking a lot of questions."

When the reporters began simply rephrasing the same tired queries, he politely said that he needed to get back to work. He turned away while they were still calling his name. Sam edged away from the cluster of microphones and followed him through the hotel's tall entry doors.

Less than halfway across the lobby she realized some of the reporters were following. She spun around and faced them.

"The festival, Sweet Somethings, is an event to raise money for charity. Unless you are here to cover that angle, you'll need to leave. Please respect our goal and please let the sheriff get on with his business."

It was the wrong thing to say. Suddenly, all of them wanted to cover the charitable aspects of the event. Sam could see a two-edged sword here—the additional publicity could very well be a detriment to Beau's investigation. On the other hand, publicity for the event and the charity could probably be a good thing. She promised a news release later in the day and the chance for their crews to film the prize awards on Sunday afternoon.

"Sorry, that's the best I can do," she responded when someone asked if Bentley Day would be available for interviews.

She headed for the ballroom, entirely sure that the reporters would lurk until, one by one, they could catch the celebrity chef and wangle interviews on their own. It was too much to hope that they would respect the department's methodical investigation rather than push for a high-profile arrest that would make national news.

She said as much to Beau a few minutes later when she caught up with him and the two had strolled past the crime scene tape in the garden, the one quiet spot on the whole property.

"We think Myrna Ulibarri started the rumor," he told her.

"The police chief's sister? She's one of our judges!" Sam remembered passing the judging stand earlier, seeing Myrna typing something on her phone. She felt her teeth grind. "I can't believe it! Of anyone in the world, families of law enforcement usually realize the harm in letting information out too early."

"I know. I know, darlin'. I've talked to her, just now. She claims she only meant to send the chief a note to let him know about the murder."

"Yeah, right. He's got all kinds of official ways to learn what he needs to know. She planted that story so her name could be associated with Bentley Day's."

"Most likely. Unfortunately, it's a bell we can't un-ring."

Oh, man, the harm that could be caused by these things. Sam stared at the trampled lawn near the rose bushes, hoping Beau's men had collected all the useful information they could get.

"Sam, I want you to be my eyes and ears inside the festival," Beau said. "If I send uniformed deputies in there, everyone who knows anything will clam up. Garcia's doing his best to ask the right questions of the right people, but they're only going to tell him so much."

"And they'll tell the sheriff's wife more?" It didn't seem likely.

"You are head of the committee and you know them all pretty well. Just try to sort through the gossip and speculation, see if you can get any actual facts that we might miss in our own questioning. That's all."

Sam had her doubts. Surely, there were other things on everyone's mind.

"Well, I better get going," Beau said. "I need to push the forensic lab to get prints from that knife, and then I better talk with the medical investigator. If the local man can't positively state the cause of death, I'll have to push Albuquerque to rush the autopsy. They won't be happy about it, on a weekend, but half our suspects are leaving town Sunday evening and I can't let this case get cold that fast." He headed for his SUV and Sam went back into the hotel, wishing she could find a moment of calm before walking into the chaotic ballroom.

Most of the action was still taking place around the judging stand. With a lull in the delivery of new entries, Bentley Day had stepped down to floor level and was posing for pictures with fans. She crossed to the second aisle, heading for her own booth. Snippets of conversation caught her attention.

"I'm not at all surprised," the chocolate chip cookie lady was saying to the one whose wares featured fragile chocolate shavings on cupcakes topped with mounds of thick frosting. "She came along yesterday afternoon at five o'clock, telling me that I had to get all my signs reprinted. I basically told her where she could shove that idea."

Farther down the line, Nancy Nash was staring out into space. Her eyes were red-rimmed and she appeared to be doing her best to avoid crying in public. When Sam looked toward her, she turned away and got busy arranging a stack of paper napkins.

Sam edged past the end of her own table, into the work area of her booth. Before she could ask Becky how things were going, Nancy leaned across the narrow space between them.

"I wish it had been Bentley Day," she whispered. "The man is such a jerk, and that woman who was killed—she was no better."

Okay, here was a good chance to get some gossip.

"Why?" Sam asked, mimicking the confidential whisper. "What did they do?"

Nancy sniffed and blinked hard. "My entry. My family's favorite recipe? He . . . he . . . laughed when he tasted it. He said it was the worst—oh, I can't even think about it. The man's a complete loser."

Sam felt for the woman. Clearly, her family either really did love the bottled syrup she used or they'd been too kind in letting her think they did. She shouldn't have been in a competition with serious chefs, true, but it wasn't a reason to publicly belittle her.

"This morning it was Carinda, watching me make my chocolate sauce, rolling her eyes and giving me this . . . this *look*. I could have—*ugh*!" She started to make a strangling motion but caught herself and let her hands drop to her sides. "Not that I would actually—"

"I know," Sam said, still whispering. "But, you know, maybe someone wasn't as gentle a person as you are . . . Did you hear anybody else say anything against her?"

"Yeah, like, everyone. I tell you, nobody liked the woman. But I can't really imagine anyone taking it that far."

Neither could Sam. She would just have to keep asking questions.

She glanced again at the dais where Bentley was still wowing the crowd with his jokes. At least the public didn't seem to be aware that a death had happened here this morning, that, or they didn't care. A quick look at the stock left in her display cases showed that over half their items had sold—and it was early afternoon of the first day.

"I better call Julio and have him ramp up the baking at the shop," she told Becky. "We'll never make it through three days with what's left here."

She stepped out to the corridor, looking for a quiet corner of the lobby to make her call. Jen assured her everything was fine at the shop, a little quiet for a Friday afternoon, but that was probably because half the town was at the festival. Sam spoke with Julio next and gave him a list of things to bake.

"I'll stop by this evening or first thing in the morning and pick them up. The show opens here at ten again tomorrow."

She hung up and suddenly felt a wave of exhaustion. Two more days of this. Where would she get the energy? Across the lobby she saw people coming out of the restaurant. Sam realized she'd completely forgotten to eat any lunch. She called Becky in the booth and offered to bring her a sandwich or something.

"I'm good, Sam. Kelly brought me something earlier. Take your time, get off your feet for a little while."

As much as she felt like a slacker for doing it, the idea held enormous appeal. She went into the restaurant where a tired-looking middle-aged hostess showed her to a table near a corner that was semi screened off from others by a divider capped with plants. The perfect spot to avoid questions, reporters and festival crises. She ordered a salad and something described as an energy smoothie.

Midway through her lunch she heard the hostess seat someone else on the other side of the divider. Great. A near-empty restaurant and the only other customer had to be right next to her. Probably something to do with the waitress's stations or the fact that she didn't want to walk across the room any more than necessary. Sam crunched a crouton, trying to drown out the sounds of the female who'd decided to place a phone call.

"I found her," said the voice. The fact that she was murmuring, an obvious attempt to keep the conversation quiet, caused Sam's ears to perk up. "But I haven't gotten the—the other thing. I can't believe Julia changed it."

Sam shifted in her seat. Unable to see the speaker, she really didn't want to be seen either. The voice was slightly familiar and she had the feeling if it was one of the vendors there would be extra conversation if she recognized Sam.

"Okay, *yeah*," said the woman. "I *will*. I'll call you." She clicked off the call with a disgusted little *puh*, then called the waitress over and asked that her order be put in a box to go.

"It's coming off the grill now. I'll tell the cook," said the waitress with one of those impatient tones that said she knew her tip would be diminished because of this.

Sam heard motion behind her as the customer got up and left. She breathed a little easier and finished her salad.

The healthful meal really had boosted her energy, as well as her mood. By the time she got back to the ballroom the judges were into a new batch of entries and even the antics of the onstage celebrity didn't bother her so much. She strolled past the booths, gauging moods, making sure the vendors were happy.

Of the ones who'd given a bit of static the previous day, Danielle Ferguson seemed a lot more subdued today.

Sam caught her sending a nervous glance toward Farrel O'Hearn's booth. Probably worried over the outcome of the competition. Danielle had openly stated that she wanted to win this thing at all cost. Did she mean that literally?

Farrel, on the other hand, seemed completely wrapped up in her own mini-celebrity status. People crowded around her booth and Sam caught more than one of them raving about the cuisine at her Santa Fe restaurant. Gone were the baleful glares from yesterday.

And Farrel wasn't the only one who seemed more relaxed with the temperamental Carinda out of the way. All over the room Sam felt a general air of fun that had been missing earlier. Did it mean that the murderer believed he or she had gotten away with it? Or was this simply because the show was underway and sales were good.

Even though Sam had committed to donate all of her three-day proceeds to their chosen charity, it wasn't mandatory and many of the vendors were probably making a good portion of their monthly income this weekend. She decided to relax and not think about the case until she'd had a chance to talk with Beau. She really had no evidence to go on anyway.

She'd circled the room by now and was about to step back into her own space.

"Sam, would you and your assistant like an ice cream cone?" Harvey Byron held up an empty cone. "On the house. Any flavor you want, as long as it's chocolate."

He smiled while the two of them decided. Becky took white chocolate raspberry, and Sam couldn't resist the chocolate chip cookie dough since she knew Harvey used an exotic Mexican vanilla in the recipe.

"Weird about Carinda, wasn't it?" he said as he dipped

out perfect globes of the creamy white chocolate flavor.

Sam nodded, working for a measure of respect toward the dead woman.

"It's too bad that no one really liked her." That was undoubtedly true, especially based on Carinda's actions of the last few days.

Harvey handed over Becky's cone and started dipping Sam's. Becky shivered and walked into their booth to serve a customer who had approached. Sam accepted her free cone and joined her. When Sam set her cone into a paper cup to bag two brownies for their customer, Becky's expression was unfathomable. The customer left and Sam's eyes met Becky's.

"It's nothing," her assistant said, giving her cone a lick. "My mother had superstitions about speaking ill of the dead. But this *is* Carinda we're talking about."

At the dais, Rupert had appeared and picked up the microphone. Sam hadn't seen him for hours and he appeared fresh enough that she suspected he had sneaked home for a nap. He'd certainly changed clothes and redone his hair. The man managed somehow to never, ever look as bedraggled as she felt right now. She sneaked a look at the time on her phone—an hour yet to go before they could shut down.

"Hello again, chocolate lovers!" Rupert said with a flourish of the purple scarf draped over his shoulder. "Does chocolate make everybody happy?"

Like filings to a magnet, the crowd shifted toward the dais, faces upturned to Rupert and the judges.

"I know everyone has been waiting to find out the names of the contestants whose entries have made it to the top ten, and to give you that delicious information . . . here is our famous Killer Chef—Bentley Day!"

Sam really needed to talk to Rupert about his choice of wording. What if it turned out to be true?

Bentley took the microphone and gave a little bow to the audience, followed by a wide smile that showed a lot of perfectly aligned teeth.

"All right, everyone—here are the finalists!"

He picked up a folded sheet of paper and began reading.

"Come up here as I call your names. Farrel O'Hearn of The Southwest Chocolatier! Harvey Byron from Ice Cream Social!"

It was a short hop for those two, to stand in front of the podium. Seven others joined in quick succession, including the brownie lady and the one with those to-die-for cupcakes. Sam avoided looking directly at Nancy Nash.

"Danielle Ferguson!"

Danielle shot Farrel a triumphant look as she took a place on the opposite end of the row.

"These contestants, ladies and gentlemen, will be further narrowed to the final five tomorrow so you want to be sure and be here for that. Besides, you will have eaten all the goodies you bought today so you'll need to come back for more, right!"

A cheer went up.

"Contestants, the pressure is on you. Bring your best recipes and take off the gloves because the battle is really on!"

Cameras flashed as the contestants posed with Bentley. Rupert reminded everyone that the doors would open again at ten in the morning and reiterated that all ticket proceeds went to charity.

"Bring your friends and make your gift shopping lists.

This is *the* place to be in Taos all weekend!"

Gradually, the gathering at the dais broke up.

"Let's organize and cover our product," Sam told Becky. "Everything will be fine here overnight, and I'll bring more from the shop. Sleep in, since Jen comes tomorrow."

"I'm used to being on my feet all day, so no problem there," Becky said. "Don's going to bring the kids by on Sunday, so I'll take a little break and walk around with them."

Sam laid a tablecloth over the open side of their display cases and tucked the zippered bag containing the money into her backpack, fishing for the keys to her van at the same time. The large room had cleared remarkably quickly, most of the vendors accustomed to trade shows where they simply draped something over their displays and beat a path out at the end of day.

In the adjacent booth, Nancy Nash was stacking plastic bowls of strawberries and looking somewhat dejected.

"I didn't sell much," she admitted. "Maybe this wasn't such a good idea."

Sam didn't know what to say. The family's kindness toward Nancy's cooking evidently hadn't been such a favor after all. She wished Nancy better luck tomorrow.

One more thing to do, she thought as she looked for Auguste Handler. He'd promised that the ballroom doors would be locked overnight and that a security guard would come by several times to be sure they stayed that way. Most of the vendors were leaving expensive equipment and a fair amount of inventory in his care. She located him behind the hotel's front desk and he assured her he had it covered.

The quickest way to her van was to take the corridor past the ballroom and go out through the garden. Near the large glass back doors she spotted the silhouette of Bentley

Day. A little girl of about seven raced ahead of Sam and called out to him.

"Mr. Chef, could I have your autograph? Please?"

Sam was twenty feet away but she heard his response.

"Bugger off, kid."

The little girl came to an abrupt halt. "What?"

"Get outta here. I'm off work until tomorrow." He lit a cigarette and pushed out to the garden.

Sam saw the stricken look on the kid's face. "Look, sweetie, I'm sorry about that. If you're here tomorrow you come by my booth for a free cupcake, okay?"

The girl nodded and trudged back toward the lobby.

"What was that?" Sam said, confronting Bentley where he leaned against an adobe pillar. "Rude to a kid? How could you think that was necessary?"

He shrugged and blew smoke toward the rose bushes. "Bloomin' wears me out sometimes. By the end of the day—"

"Drop the accent. You're off work until tomorrow." She stalked away to her van. What a complete rat!

Chapter 12

A frozen casserole would have to suffice for dinner. Sam felt no guilt whatsoever as she pulled the packaged entrée from the freezer, read the directions and stuck the cheap aluminum pan into the oven. A shower and a glass of wine . . . she might begin to feel human.

She thought again of Sarah, lying in the hospital and how the final encounter with Bentley the chef had capped an already stressful day; she found herself replaying it while the hot water poured over her head. As she scrubbed shampoo into her scalp she forced her thoughts away from the obnoxious celebrity. But then her mind began to go back over the rest of the day's events—Carinda's body lying in the garden behind the hotel, the questions from Beau's investigator, the petty emotional turmoil surrounding the competitors at the festival. How could grownups get so worked up over recipes? And that thought led her back to, how could a grown man treat a little kid so rudely? She rinsed away the suds, determined to put all that behind her for the rest of the evening.

By the time she walked downstairs, wearing comfy capris and a loose top, the smell of chicken and green chile was beginning to fill the house. Maybe the casserole idea wasn't such a bad one.

"Hey, darlin'," Beau said, coming through the front door just in time to deliver a kiss.

"You look the way I felt thirty minutes ago," she teased. "Dinner can be ready anytime, so grab a shower first if you want."

He rested his chin on her head and drew a long breath. "You do smell a lot better than me. I'll take you up on that offer."

By the time he emerged, she'd set the table and made a salad to go along with the pasta, chicken and chile combination. He pulled a beer from the fridge. Sam plopped into her chair, hoping the meal would revive her.

"So . . . long day, huh." She watched as he scooped up a huge portion of the casserole.

"Seems that way. The latest was a report of a grass fire up north. Not that my department has to deal with it, but we get notified along with every other agency. BLM dispatched some firefighters. I'm just hoping it doesn't spread. There's no forecast of rain in sight."

Poor thing—Sam felt for him—too many things to keep track of.

"But I assume what you really want to know is whether we've figured out who killed Carinda Carter." He smiled at her, knowing that she didn't expect an answer this early on.

It never went quite that easily.

"I can tell you that the knife was covered in prints. We identified Carinda's and Bentley Day's."

Not surprising.

"But there were a zillion others, none that we could identify."

"Anyone involved in setting up the festival could have had access to it," she told him. "Plus who knows who might have touched it before Bentley even brought it to town."

"You're right. I'm afraid the weapon might not reveal much, from that standpoint."

Sam sipped her wine.

"The autopsy results . . . not all that helpful either," Beau said. "The cause of death was definitely the knife wound. The killer only had to take one stab at it, so to speak. Death was instantaneous and probably happened only shortly before the body was found. The whole thing probably transpired in a few seconds and the person just kept on walking."

Coolly enough to walk right back into the ballroom and proceed to sell chocolates all day? Or to host the show as though nothing at all was wrong? It would take a hard heart and a lot of acting skill to pull that off.

"Bentley was out of sight when the murder happened," Sam said after telling Beau how rude the man had been at the end of the day. "And he had another knife handy so the show could go on."

"A fact that no one else probably knew—in case the killer planned to frame him by using his knife. You did say that it was in a box in the ballroom where at least fifty people had access to it."

"Carinda had insulted a couple of the contestants.

The previous day she made remarks about the school
Farrel O'Hearn attended—called the place a pretentious,
overpriced mill for short-order cooks."

"She said that directly to Ms. O'Hearn?"

"No. She muttered it to Kelly, but I'm sure Farrel
overheard. She was staring daggers—uh, sorry, bad choice
of words. She gave Carinda hateful looks all afternoon.
Still, she would have had to harbor that anger overnight and
show up full of rage the next morning."

"It's been known to happen."

He offered to clear the plates. Sam picked up the serving
bowls and followed him to the kitchen.

"Nancy Nash was another one Carinda insulted by
saying her chocolate-dipped strawberries could be made by
a four-year-old."

"Ouch."

"Actually, they probably could, but anyone with a degree
of politeness wouldn't say so." She pulled a carton of ice
cream from the freezer and found bowls. "Really, the only
person there who seems too nice to have hated Carinda is
Harvey Byron. The ice cream guy. He somehow manages to
put a positive spin on everything."

Beau wiggled his eyebrows. "It's the nice ones who'll
fool you."

Sam shut him up by handing him a bowl and spoon.
She leaned a hip against the kitchen counter and dug into
her own.

"Does that include my own friends?" Sam asked after
her first spoonful of butter pecan. "Because everyone—
Kelly, Riki, Rupert—they were all milling around. Things
were such a madhouse this morning, anyone could have

followed Carinda out the back door."

She recalled looking for Rupert right before the show opened, since he was to make the announcements. Neither he nor Bentley had been in the ballroom. But he had come in minutes before ten.

Beau interrupted that line of thinking. "For now, aside from figuring out who did the crime, we're looking for Carinda Carter's next of kin. There's not a lot to go on. We found her purse, locked away in the trunk of her car. She still had an out-of-state license, but all I've gotten from that is verification that she had no criminal record and she hadn't yet made New Mexico her permanent residence."

"What state did she come from?"

"New York. I don't have any personal contacts there so all my queries have to go through channels. It may be days before we get anything substantial."

"She lived in an apartment in town. There's probably some personal correspondence or something, maybe an address book."

Beau finished his ice cream and set the bowl in the sink. "Yeah, we'll get to that soon. Meanwhile—" He let out a huge yawn.

"We should get to bed early. I have to go by the shop in the morning and pick up more stuff that Julio baked. We actually made a lot of sales today, in spite of all this other."

Sam put the last of the dishes into the dishwasher while he walked out to the front porch with the dogs. Fifteen minutes later, with all of them safely inside, they went upstairs. Sam lay in the dark, hunting for that pleasant state of doziness but mainly plagued by scenes from the day that kept rolling through her mind.

Carinda marching through the ballroom, tossing last-minute orders out to the vendors, passing by Farrel O'Hearn's booth, two flashes of the same shade of blue. Sam's eyes flew open. She hadn't made the connection before this very minute. O'Hearn was wearing a blue dress, too, form fitting, a bit low cut, very similar to Carinda's. Both women were slender, both had reddish hair cut about the same length. The prestigious chef had no shortage of enemies. Danielle Ferguson was chief among them. But she'd battled with Carinda and had belittled a couple of the other contestants as well.

What if Carinda had not been the intended victim at all? What if someone had really been after Farrel O'Hearn?

Sam rolled over to tell Beau about her idea but he was snoring softly on his side of the bed and she didn't have the heart to wake him. He would be only too happy to hear her theory tomorrow rather than tonight. She closed her eyes again but images of the festival continued to fill her head. Was there anyone among the crowd who seemed uneasy, edgy, afraid of being caught? She found herself in an endless loop, rehashing everything she and Beau had discussed over dinner, frustrated that her mind would not shut down.

When her alarm rang at four-thirty, she felt as if she'd had no more than an hour's sleep all night. She dragged herself to the bathroom where she quietly slipped into her work clothes and brushed her teeth, trying not to wake Beau.

Sweet's Sweets looked a little forlorn and Sam realized her shop had missed having her own touch. She neatened the window display and beverage bar in the sales room, then visited her desk where notes and bits of stuff that didn't have any better place always seemed to end up. She filed some receipts, paid a couple of bills, and went to the website of her main supplier to replenish her stock of flour, sugar and butter.

The baked items for the festival, which Julio had finished yesterday afternoon, waited in neat boxes on the worktable. She peeked in and helped herself to a couple of cookies. *I've got to stop doing this—sneaking treats in lieu of breakfast; I'll never lose these extra pounds.*

She stuck the second cookie into her desk drawer—as if it might vanish from there and never tempt her again. The back doorknob rattled and Becky came in.

"Ready for another day," she said. "Although, I tell you, I completely crashed when I got home last night. Don got the boys a pizza and put them to bed, on his own."

"Feel free to close the shop a little early if things are slow," Sam said. "If it's like yesterday, most of our customers will have found us at the festival."

Becky nodded and picked up the stack of order forms. "I want to finish any special order items before seven. Most likely I won't get back into the kitchen once the Open sign turns over."

The noisy sound of a motorcycle came from the alley and Julio appeared within a couple of minutes. The three of them loaded the bakery boxes into Sam's van.

"Okay, looks like you two have this under control," Sam said. "I'm going to head out."

What she really wanted was a decent breakfast before spending the day surrounded by tempting sweets. It wasn't too early anymore to call Beau so she got into her van and dialed his cell. He suggested they meet in the restaurant at Bella Vista.

Probably not the best idea, as it turned out. Sam started

to tell him her idea that Farrel O'Hearn might have been the intended victim, but then she realized the restaurant was quickly filling up with other people from the festival. They ordered eggs and kept their conversation neutral.

Sam was struggling to resist slathering jam over her healthy whole-wheat toast when Beau's phone chirped to signal an incoming text. He read it quickly and sighed.

"Looks like I need to check with my dispatcher. I'll step outside. It's fine if the server wants to take my plate. I'm probably leaving anyway."

It was all Sam needed to pass up the toast. She signaled for the check as he walked out. By the time she'd paid their tab she saw that he was sitting in his cruiser, parked near the high portico. She walked out to say goodbye.

"It's the peace-and-love bunch. Looks like things got a little rowdy overnight and we may have to hand out some citations for use of fun-but-illegal substances. Rico's there but he can use some help. I still have a lot of people to question here, too. Ben Garcia and I will be back after awhile."

"I'll be here all day," Sam told him. "I can keep my ears open on the Carinda situation, if you'd like."

"Keep an open mind, darlin'. It could turn out to be someone completely outside the festival."

She nodded. Down inside, she knew that. But so much of Carinda's life had revolved, in recent days, around the events of the weekend. It seemed a little farfetched that she died here if the murder had nothing to do with anyone in this crowd. She watched Beau drive away, more determined than ever to learn what she could about all the players.

A line had already formed in front of the ticket table and Sam realized the doors would open to the public in another ten minutes.

When she entered the ballroom, the first thing she noticed was that Farrel O'Hearn was not in her booth. If Farrel was the intended victim yesterday, she could still be on someone's radar. Sam quickly took inventory: Rupert was chatting with the two lady judges on the dais; Bentley Day was not there yet, but that probably was no surprise—he'd done the late-appearance thing yesterday; Kelly and Jen were already in the Sweet's Sweets booth, uncovering the tables and adding new stock to the display; Danielle Ferguson was in her own booth, seemingly occupied with her wares, as were the vendors in all the other booths. Except for Nancy Nash. Her crock pot and strawberries were gone. Evidently, the hurt feelings went deep and she'd decided her time as a festival vendor was over.

Rupert picked up the microphone, as he had yesterday, welcomed the vendors and repeated the instructions for submitting their entries to the judges. Today's entry must be something different than yesterday's and must be sent to the front anonymously—and good luck to everyone.

The doors opened and the crowd poured in.

Sweet's Sweets immediately became busy. Word had obviously gotten out about Sam's amaretto cheesecake because they had four requests for it within fifteen minutes.

"I'm going to sneak out back and phone Julio," Sam said to Jen. "At this rate, we'll need more of these before the day is over."

She hurried out and made the call, coming back to find that Kelly had been pulled away to deliver contest entries to the judges and Jen was a little swamped. Together, they sold boxes of molded chocolates and bags of cookies and brownies at a frantic pace for two hours.

At the west end of the room, Sam was slightly aware of Bentley Day's arrival and his antics with the microphone but, frankly, she no longer saw his charm. If it turned out that Beau proved him to be a killer, it wouldn't sadden her a bit.

Somewhere around noon, they noticed a lull in the size of the crowd.

"Finally, a chance to check things and neaten up our stock," Jen said quietly, after sending a woman and her little girl off with smiles and cupcakes. "This is wild. At the shop I'm used to having enough quiet moments to keep the place cleaned up."

Sam chuckled. "Yeah, the whole atmosphere of a festival is really—" Her phone buzzed and interrupted that thought.

She stole a glance at the readout; the number was somewhat familiar but she couldn't quite place it.

"Sam, hello. It's Marc Williams." His voice was hollow and Sam guessed the bad news even before he delivered it. She signaled to Jen that she would be right back.

"It's Sarah?" she asked, her eyes welling up as she pushed her way out of the ballroom and found a deserted pathway into the garden.

"Yes. I'm afraid she had a fatal stroke early this morning."

Sam felt herself deflate. "I'm *so* sorry. We're really going to miss her."

"Right before the end, my aunt regained consciousness and actually spoke a little. She wanted you here but it was rather late last night. I told her I would call you in the morning. I should have tried sooner . . . I'm really sorry I didn't. If I'd realized at the time, I think she was saying goodbye."

"Oh, Marc—" Words seemed so useless—they didn't change anything.

"Sam, do you know a historian named Doctor St. Clair? A woman. I got the impression she might be connected to a wooden box that Aunt Sarah spoke about."

The name meant nothing to Sam. "Did Sarah talk about this box as she was dying?"

"No, not really. A mention of it, then she asked if you were nearby—otherwise it was only family things. I'm sorry, Sam. I wish I knew more. I just wanted to let you know about Sarah."

She thanked Marc and asked about funeral services. Tuesday, he said, and she promised to get in touch again as soon as her festival duties were over. She hung up, feeling the weight of the loss. There had been so much left unsaid. She would always regret that she had not known Sarah better.

Chapter 13

Sam dropped her phone back into her pocket and looked up to see Beau's cruiser pulling into the parking lot. She swallowed the lump of sadness over the news of Sarah's death and walked toward her handsome husband.

"How did it go?" she asked when he joined her at the sidewalk near the place where the vendors had unloaded their wares Thursday afternoon.

He lifted a shoulder. "Okay. No arrests, just a bunch of warnings. I couldn't see the use of going after warrants to find out that Moondoggie and his bunch keep stashes of pot in their buses. This murder case takes precedence, so Ben Garcia is joining me to conduct more interrogations. Want to sit in?"

True to plan, Garcia's vehicle wheeled in and parked next to Beau's.

"Let me check on my booth real quick. I ducked out to take a phone call a few minutes ago." She told him about Sarah's death, but since he'd not known the woman and the death wasn't suspicious, his interest quickly turned back to his real purpose.

"We'll be in the same room Garcia used yesterday," he said as they parted in the corridor.

Behind their small sales counter, Kelly and Jen seemed to have things under control. A Sold tag leaned beside the bathtub cake.

"Yeah, a lady who is hosting a bridal shower tomorrow afternoon," Jen said. "She raved over this cake—said it was perfect for her group. I guess they are all into spa weekends and such. She wanted to take it with her now but I told her we wouldn't let it get away. She was okay with that. I think she wanted to spend a little time indulging in more chocolate anyway. She did pay for it."

"Mom? Everything okay?" Kelly asked.

Sam told them about Sarah Williams. "I wish she could have been here to see how well the festival turned out. I'll try to pass the word quietly to the rest of the committee."

The girls nodded and a customer walked up, pulling Jen's attention to the cookie selection in the display case.

"Beau and Garcia are here," Sam murmured to Kelly. "If you girls can handle things in the booth, I think I'll go see how their work is coming along."

"This is about Carinda?"

"Yeah. They seem to have too many suspects and not enough solid leads at this point. They're re-interviewing people from yesterday, so don't be surprised if they call you in."

Kelly shrugged. "Not a problem."

Sam made her way through the crowded ballroom without getting hooked into conversation and took the stairs to the second floor. The door to the suite stood open and she spotted Beau in the same chair where Ben Garcia sat yesterday. She tapped at the door and walked in.

"You two learning anything new yet?" she teased.

"Just getting organized. Ben went to the ballroom to bring up our first witness. We're starting with Bentley Day and working our way through everyone else connected with the festival."

"Are you sure I should be here?"

"It's fine. I always appreciate your take on the interrogations. You didn't, by chance, handle that little—" His hands formed a square that indicated the size and shape of the carved box. Although Beau didn't know exactly how the object affected Sam, there were times when she'd been able to tell that someone was lying. Once, she'd even spotted invisible toxic dust inside a house that carried fingerprints, where the lawmen hadn't thought to dust for them.

"Sorry, no. I didn't think of it today."

"Well, if your aura-vision or whatever you call it should happen to go on alert around any of our suspects, you be sure and let me know."

"Right."

Voices in the hallway caught their attention before Ben Garcia and Bentley Day stepped into view. Once inside, Garcia closed the door and ushered the celebrity chef into the small living room setting. Bentley eyed Sam for a moment. Other than the confrontation over his rudeness toward that young girl last evening, she'd never had a real conversation with the man and he seemed a little confused as to what her role really was. Oh well, let him wonder.

He settled on the couch when the two lawmen took the upholstered chairs; Sam stood with a shoulder against the wall, taking a spot at the edge of the room near the small dining table.

"I know you are busy, Mr. Day," Garcia began. "Thanks for taking a few minutes to help us out."

"Dunno what you want," Bentley said. "I answered everything yesterday."

"Can you go over it again, for my benefit," said Beau, "since I wasn't in the room then."

Bentley gave an impatient sigh.

"*And* since your very-identifiable knife was used to commit the murder." Beau gave him a firm stare.

Day's attitude receded marginally. "I told your detective—I was in my room on the third floor. Checked in Thursday evening, hung out in the bar awhile and chatted up this cute girl. Monica, I think her name was, but I have to admit that I don't really remember. We ended up in my room. She left maybe one o'clock or so. I slept like a real happy man until nearly ten o'clock when someone came along and pounded on the door to wake me up."

"Who was that?"

"The woman. The dead one."

"Did you let her into your room?"

"I met her at the door, wearing nothing at all. She seemed a little surprised—maybe she was impressed, hell if I know."

"Did she come into your room?"

"Nah. Got a little flustered, said they wanted me downstairs, would I please get my clothes on and get to the festival. I said sure. She wasn't my type anyway—I like women with some curves to them. Last I saw of that one she was beating a path toward the elevator."

"How long before you went down to the ballroom?"

"Fifteen, twenty minutes? Thereabouts. I go into my routine, wow the crowd . . . you know."

"Did you see Carinda Carter before you went to the ballroom? Maybe you agreed to meet her in the garden before show time?"

"Nope. Not interested, like I told you." Bentley fiddled with his watchband as he spoke.

Sam wasn't sure she believed the line about Carinda not being his type. From what she'd seen of Bentley and his continuous flirting with the women in the crowd, it didn't seem there was any female who wasn't his type.

"Did you see Carinda after you went to the ballroom?" Garcia asked.

"No! Man, that's just gross. The woman was dead by then, wasn't she? What would I want with that?"

That much was true—Bentley had been on the dais, in full limelight when Carinda's body was found. Garcia leaned toward Beau, showing him something written on his small notebook. If the goal was to make their suspect nervous, it worked. Bentley fidgeted in his seat but that might have been solely because he wanted to get back to the throngs of eager women downstairs. Beau dismissed him with a caution not to leave town without their permission.

When the door closed behind Day, Beau turned to Sam. "What do you think, does the timeframe fit?"

She thought back to the hectic morning. "Once the doors opened and people began to come in, I got pretty busy. But it seems more than fifteen or twenty minutes went by from when Carinda went looking for Bentley and when he made his flashy appearance on stage."

"So he might have had time to get dressed and follow her to the garden?"

"You only have his word for it that he greeted Carinda at his own door stark naked. If he was dressed when she arrived, sure, there would have been plenty of time."

Garcia piped up: "The man was wearing chef whites when I interviewed him yesterday and they were spotless."

"And," Beau added, "we have to look at motive. What could have enraged him so quickly?"

Sam thought back to the numerous other people Carinda had managed to antagonize in short order. "What if the rest of Bentley's story is fake, too? The woman he took up to his room the night before—what if it wasn't a random hook-up? It could have been Carinda. She was certainly enamored of his celebrity status and she might have showed up at the bar. Given several hours together, yeah, I could see the anger begin to flare."

Beau keyed his radio and got through to Rico. "Find out who was bartending here at the hotel last night. If he or she remembers Bentley Day picking up a woman, bring the bartender up here."

"There would be DNA or some other evidence in his room," Garcia suggested.

"But if the sheets were changed and the room vacuumed yesterday morning, it's probably all gone. We didn't have any reason to tell housekeeping not to clean the guest rooms at ten o'clock yesterday morning."

That aspect of it seemed a dead end, Sam had to admit.

"Let's take a look at Carinda's other enemies. Remember, anyone in the place could have gotten hold of the knife." Beau flipped to a new page in his notebook. "Sam, you were there. Who else left the ballroom right before the show opened?"

She searched back in her memory. "Farrell O'Hearn wasn't in her booth. I remember that because it seemed odd that her assistant had the place, right before the crowds were due to come in. Danielle Ferguson had a row with Carinda over her booth location, but that was the previous afternoon and I thought it got settled to everyone's satisfaction. Danielle did leave the room that morning, though, and when she returned she seemed agitated."

"What about your committee members, Sam? I know you don't want to think badly of any one of them but they did have the most contact with Carinda, the longer history."

"Let's just say that no one was a fan, myself included. She and Rupert got crossways at our last meeting. The worst Harvey ever did was send her a firm look whenever she gave him one of her glares. Kelly and Riki mostly ignored her."

"Where were each of them at the time Carinda was killed?" Beau asked.

"Kelly and Becky were helping me with my booth. Riki's been busy with her grooming shop and hasn't been around the hotel at all. Harvey is running his ice cream stand. I don't recall any particular friction between him and Carinda after we got it settled that she didn't have the right to assign booth spaces—at one point she'd tried to put his booth outdoors in the sun. That didn't go over too well."

A tap at the door and Rico came in. "Sheriff, I located the bartender on duty last night. She's a friendly type who seems to chat up the patrons. She remembered Bentley Day coming in Thursday evening, ordering a Scotch, neat. But she doesn't at all recall him leaving with a woman. Says things got a little busy around nine so she can't swear to it, just that she didn't recall anybody with Mr. Day."

"Thanks, Rico."

"I brought Mr. Penrick with me," Rico said with a tilt of his head toward the door.

Rupert came in as Rico left, reeking of impatience until he spotted Sam.

"What's this about?" he asked as he sat across from the two lawmen.

"Routine questions, Rupert," Beau said. "We're only trying to figure out where everyone was at the time Carinda Carter was killed."

"He did that yesterday," said Rupert, nodding toward Ben Garcia.

"I know, and we appreciate your statement. Sometimes new information comes in that requires a little clarification. We understand that you left the ballroom for awhile right before the festival officially opened."

"Yes. Last-minute pit-stop, okay? Everyone needs those."

Beau shuffled in his seat. "True. Did you see Bentley Day around that time, outside the ballroom?"

"I did not. I would have ordered the man to his post because everything was running a bit behind schedule by then."

"You had an altercation with the victim just before that, something about the girls taking tickets?"

Rupert gave Sam a withering glance.

"It wasn't exactly a fight," he said. "The woman butted into every small aspect of the show and I was only one of many who resented her intrusion. Clearly, I should not have voiced that opinion to the wife of the sheriff."

Sam crossed the room and sat beside Rupert on the

small sofa. "Rupe, don't be this way. I didn't say that you harmed Carinda. There's no way I would think such a thing."

"Settle down, Mr. Penrick," Ben Garcia said. "We're just trying to get a picture here. While you were outside the ballroom, did you see anyone go out the back doors toward the garden? Carinda Carter or anyone else?"

"No. Of course there were so many people milling about, most of them making their way to their booths . . . truthfully, I wasn't looking for anyone other than Bentley Day at that point. He lollygagged around his room until the last minute, apparently, because Sam and I had to start the announcements ourselves. Our *celebrity* didn't bother to show up until it was nearly time for the judging to begin."

Sam nodded. She remembered Bentley's obnoxious chopping routine and ill-timed act with one of his knives. His clothes had indeed been spotless, but there had certainly been time for him to rush back to his room for a change before anyone actually saw him in public. Carinda's version of meeting Bentley and going up to his room to remind him about coming downstairs didn't exactly gel with his story, but what would have been the star chef's motive to get rid of her?

Chapter 14

In the elevator she took Rupert's hand. "I swear, Beau does not consider you a suspect," she said. "He has to ask everyone about their movements so he can put together what happened."

He squeezed her fingers. "I know, Sam. I'm not blaming."

Sam's eyes watered up as her mind switched gears.

"Hey, it's okay," he said.

"I didn't get the chance to tell you—Sarah died, in the early hours this morning."

"I'm so sorry, girl. We all really liked her. I'll plan to go to the funeral and I can tell some of the others on the committee about it."

"Thanks." Sam patted his shoulder.

In the corridor, things were a little quieter than before. Rupert paused to speak with the judges, discussing the opportune time to call for the next few entries in the chocolate contest and spark things up again. Most of the booths had a few customers and a fresh batch of twenty-somethings hovered near the dais, cute girls in tight tops who were flirting outrageously with Bentley Day. He gave Sam a long glance then immediately turned his attention back to a young brunette in hot pink.

Sam paused in front of the ice cream cart to pass along the news about Sarah to Harvey. He expressed sincere condolences, then became distracted by a woman signaling him across the room. In the Sweet's Sweets booth Kelly finished ringing up a sale for a man with a cup of coffee in his hand and suggested the garden as a nice place to sit with his dessert. She and Jen both repeated Rupert's sentiments when they heard about Sarah.

Sam mindlessly flipped through the cash bag, in case they needed change, wishing she had someone to talk to about the fact that the older woman had died before they got the chance to talk about the one subject foremost on Sam's mind, the mysterious wooden box. Maybe later at home with Beau. She picked up a broken cookie and ate half of it in one bite.

"Boy, this is weird," Kelly said, looking up from her copy of *People*, which she had opened to a random page. "Some wealthy woman threatened to leave forty billion dollars to her dog after all her other heirs pissed her off."

Jen glanced over Kelly's shoulder. "Oh, yeah. Julia Joffrey. I heard about that. She died a few months ago, didn't she?"

As usual, when it came to celebrities and the surrounding gossip, Sam felt out of the loop.

Jen eyed Bentley Day, now up on the dais making an

announcement that the last three contestants should send their entries forward for judging.

"I'll bet he knew Julia Joffrey," she said. "Remember that other show he starred in, before *Killer Chef*? It took place in Washington and there was always some socialite or famous person who would come to the restaurant for the meal he prepared."

"Yes!" Kelly lit up. "I think I actually remember that one. She was this society type from Maryland or someplace, seemed ancient—but she dressed really classy and Bentley teased her the whole time."

"He teased everyone the whole time. I think it's how he tried out the semi-obnoxious personality he uses now."

Semi? Sam hid a smile.

"Did he have the Australian accent back then?"

"Hmm, I think so. Maybe not as strong as it is now." Kelly tossed the magazine aside as two kids approached and held up a dollar bill. She saw to it that they got a decent-sized bag of cookies for their money.

"Cute, huh." She looked toward Sam. "Mom, do you realize that we need more cheesecake?"

"Again?" Sam stared at the round cardboard base with one remaining slice. I called Julio earlier and asked him to bake more. Tomorrow's only a half-day here and I'm sure things will be winding down early. We'll have to make do with what we have and I'll go by the shop on my way home tonight to get them."

As if they'd heard of a run on a failing bank, two people stepped up and split the final slice.

Jen waited on them while Sam checked the other items in the display. She *really* did not want to spend the night baking, but there might not be any other time.

"Sam, I've got Julio on the phone—he says he's got one cheesecake already done. Do you want more than that?" Jen held the phone away from her ear while she waited for Sam's answer.

"Tell him yes, two more. I'll go to the shop right now for the finished one and we'll use the others for tomorrow."

Up on the dais, Rupert was calling out names of people whose tickets had been drawn for door prizes. The room had somehow filled up again.

"I'll be back in fifteen minutes. Anyone dying for cheesecake can have some then," Sam said as she picked up her pack and headed for the parking lot. In the corridor she caught sight of the ice cream guy deep in conversation with the tall blonde who'd been at his booth earlier. A little festival romance? She smiled and hurried on.

At Sweet's Sweets Sam noted that the kitchen was clean and Julio already had the two extra cheesecakes in the oven. Becky sat at one of the bistro tables, chatting with three women who were taking their time over afternoon coffee and cake. She came to the register and gave Sam a quick rundown of the morning sales.

With the spare amaretto cheesecake in hand, Sam went back out to her van. She'd hardly unlocked the door when a large form appeared beside her. Her heart raced into overdrive.

"Bobul!" She gripped the bakery box. "What are you—?"

"Good day, Miss Samantha. Sorry. Bobul not mean to scare."

Everything about him was the same as the last time she'd seen him—his hulking six-foot frame in rough clothing, thick facial features and delicate hands—even down to the heavy boots and long, dark coat that must feel oppressive in the June heat. She'd learned that he came from Romania as a child but could only guess how many other places he had traveled before showing up in almost this exact spot two Christmases ago and offering his help. His exquisite chocolate creations had helped launch her sales into the stratosphere during her first holiday season. She had no idea where he called home, certainly not the abandoned cabin in the canyon where he'd been staying while he worked for her; as far as she could tell, he lived nowhere in this county. The man seemed to arrive and disappear on the ether. Now, she could only guess that he had somehow heard of the chocolate festival.

"Do you need a job?" Half hoping he would say yes and she would immediately put him to work on something that could become her grand finale for the event.

He shook his head vigorously. "Bobul come to warn you."

"Warn me of wh—"

He held up a hand. "We talk, long time ago, about bad people who want—" he glanced up and down the alley and stared at the closed door to her shop. "Carved box. Bad people want that box still."

Sam's mind shifted gears. Her last mention of the box to anyone was to Sarah Williams.

"Persons will come. They want box. Do not trust."

Sarah had not asked to have the box.

"A good person will also come. This one not asking for box, only want to know it is safe. This person looking for other box, the evil one."

An evil person? Or an evil box? Sam started to open her mouth but he spoke again, quickly.

"Bobul learn there is more than one box."

Sam knew that much. She had encountered the second one last fall in Ireland, in her uncle's possession.

"Bobul—I want to know the whole story. Can we meet somewhere later? Can you tell me all of it?"

He shook his head and ignored her questions. "One is bad. One good. Good person will say these words to you." He looked skyward, working to get it right. "Will say 'lightning strikes once and makes three'."

Sam repeated the phrase, but there were so many thoughts coursing through her head at the moment that she doubted she would remember it exactly.

"Bobul, please come back tomorrow—or even tonight. I need to ask more about this."

"Is all Bobul know. I must go now."

She watched him walk away, started to run after him but paused. He'd always been a man of few words and he probably wouldn't tell her anything new even if she hounded him. She ran the odd phrase through her mind again as she set the boxed cheesecake on the passenger seat of her van.

A deep sigh escaped her. Too many questions, not enough answers. Too many deaths. Too little sleep.

That was it, she decided as she put the van in gear and pulled out into traffic. She was simply tired. Get through today; finish the festival tomorrow. Sleep for a week. It wouldn't happen but it sounded so good that it buoyed her mood.

She had lost her parking spot under the trees and had to settle for a less appealing one in full sun. Inside, the crowd seemed denser than ever and she realized it was nearly time for the announcement of the 'final five' as Rupert had been referring to the contestants who would make the cut today. Sam found that a small queue had formed, people waiting for the new cheesecake Kelly had promised. She set it down and Kelly began selling the slices; within minutes it was more than half gone.

Sam moved about the booth on automatic, filling orders, shifting items in the display case, opening a new pack of napkins and setting more paper bags near the register. For Jen, waiting on customers came as second nature and she efficiently kept the ranks of people moving happily along with their purchases. Kelly excused herself to go up to the dais; the announcement of the second-round contestants would be made soon. Rupert was nowhere to be seen, probably hidden away someplace, tallying the ballots.

Sam barely gave any of this a passing thought, her mind still reliving the strange encounter with Bobul an hour ago.

There was something unexplainable about that box, and each time Sam felt she was coming close to the answer it eluded her. Again today, Bobul dropped hints but didn't give the full answers. Perhaps it was as he'd said—he simply didn't know. But, lightning? Lightning strikes once and makes three—what did that mean? It sounded as if he was warning her of real danger. She shivered, staring for a moment at the elaborate ceiling in the ballroom; if only someone would come along who could tell her.

That line of thinking led her back to Sarah Williams. The healer had been the last in a succession of people whom Sam had hoped could tell her what the mysterious gift was all about and now Sarah was gone. She'd lost the answers and she'd lost a friend.

Rupert's voice from the podium interrupted her

downward-spiraling thoughts.

"Welcome, everyone!" he called out. "The judges have tasted today's scrumptious dessert entries, they've marked their ballots, the votes have been tallied . . . And now, to announce the names of the five finalists, here is our celebrity judge, Mr. Bentley Day, the host of *Killer Chef*!"

Bentley came on full force again, striding across the tiny stage with arms upraised, slashing through the air with that repulsive knife to the calls of "Chop Chop!" from the crowd. Sam looked away, tired of the whole showmanship game.

"G'day!" he shouted.

The crowd poured toward the stage. If the ballroom had been a ship, the thing would have listed to that end. For one ridiculous moment Sam pictured all the booths and tables sliding to that part of the room. She caught herself chuckling at the image.

"All right! Here are your finalists, based on the number of points given by the judges. In fifth place . . . Susan Sanchez with her Molten Lava Volcano Cake! Susan, come on up here."

The plump little woman seemed surprised but hurried to the dais.

"In fourth place, Cynthia Freeman with Bitter Chocolate English Butter Toffee! Get over here, Cynthia."

Sam knew the lady as a customer of her shop, but never had an inkling that Cynthia was a pretty extraordinary cook.

"And now, for the top three . . ."

He dragged out the announcement and Sam saw that both Farrel O'Hearn and Danielle Ferguson seemed to be balancing on the balls of their feet.

"In third place, Grace Maldonado with Dark Chocolate

Raspberry Tarts!" He waved the lady toward him, to a huge cheer from the crowd. Apparently she'd brought along her own fan club.

"And now . . . for the top two. Any guesses as to who they might be?"

Oh, come on, Sam thought. They have to be Danielle and Farrel. Then the thought struck her—if the next name he called was not one of those two, there was likely to be another murder right here on the spot. This time it might be their grandstanding celebrity chef who went down.

But, rather predictably, the top two were Farrel and Danielle—in that order. Farrel sent a triumphant little brushoff glance to Danielle as she took the number one spot on the stand. Danielle retaliated with a clenched jaw and icy smile. The war was definitely on.

"All right, ladies," Bentley said. "Remember that tomorrow's entry must be something entirely new. And the judges will be looking not only at taste and presentation, but we shall be giving favor to the entry most stunning in the elaborately decorated department. Have at it, and may the best baker win!"

You could charge batteries on the amount of electricity sparking between the two top rivals. The other women's emotions ranged from stunned to nervous to exuberant as they descended the steps and were surrounded by their own friends in the crowd.

The big announcement had capped the day's events for most people and Sam noticed a steady flow out the doors. She left her booth in the capable hands of Kelly and Jen, while she made one last pass through the ballroom. Some of the vendors were obviously packing up their wares—the contest itself had been their only goal; others seemed to have taken Sam's strategy—sell all you could in three days—whether it be for charity, as in her case, or just to make extra money and gain visibility in the community.

Danielle Ferguson was back in her booth, sketching something on a pad which she set face down on the table as Sam approached. Her design for tomorrow's grand finale?

"Congratulations, Danielle. Good luck tomorrow," Sam said.

"So you think I'll beat Farrel?"

Sam shrugged. "I have no idea. I don't get a vote. I'm just thankful that we're getting good crowds. It looks like we'll have a decent donation for our charity."

Danielle made all the right sounds about the charity but still, underlying her thin attempts at good sportsmanship, her deep hunger to win showed through.

Sam moved on, wishing again for Sarah's steadying presence, sad that their friendship had ended so abruptly and that Sarah had missed the excitement of the festival, the fruits of all her hard work.

Two other vendors interrupted Sam with questions which she answered absently, wondering where Beau was right now. Sweet's Sweets had sold so much of their product that she realized she'd better plan on going back and baking some more. Sunday might be a slower sales day but she didn't want her offerings to look skimpy. Kelly had done a good job of getting press coverage for the event and with the announcement of the prizes tomorrow, there would likely be a sizeable crowd.

"Yeah, I knew the old bat," Farrel O'Hearn was saying to someone at her booth, keeping her voice low as Sam passed by.

Sam looked up to see Farrel toss something onto the

back table in her booth, the same copy of *People*, open to the page Kelly had showed her earlier about the peculiar heiress who'd left a fortune to her dog. Was that who Farrel was talking about? Sam shrugged it off. Farrel made no secret of the fact that she'd gotten her training in some high-class east coast place. It was a little disconcerting to hear her talk of the society woman in such disparaging terms, but that seemed to be Farrel's way. Sam could only imagine how she thought of the hicks from the Southwest.

She headed toward the dais to remind Rupert and Bentley that tomorrow's schedule would be tightened; rather than being open from ten in the morning to five p.m., it would close with the finale announcement of the prize winners at two o'clock. She had no sooner passed that info along than her phone rang. When she saw who it was she detoured to take the call at the quiet end of the corridor.

"Hey, darlin'," said Beau. "Just checking in. Are you getting out of there anytime soon?"

"I'll make it happen. I'm anxious to hear about the rest of your day."

"I left Ben to finish questioning witnesses. I'm still trying to locate next of kin for Carinda Carter and there hasn't been a minute all day to break away and get by her apartment to look for names. So, what I was thinking is that if I can swing by and pick you up, we could do that together and I'll take you out for your favorite enchiladas at the Taoseño."

It was too good an offer to pass up and Sam told him she could be ready in fifteen minutes. She scurried back to her booth, jotted quick notes about the products they'd run out of (telling Beau she would have to go to the shop and bake tonight was unwelcome news she would save for later), then she sent the girls home and was waiting in front of the hotel when Beau pulled up, right on time.

Chapter 15

Hey there," he said with a small romantic leer to his voice. "I am so ready to get this day finished and go home to relax."

She broke the news about having to bake some more; his hopeful expression faded.

"Just one more day of this," she said, "and I promise— we will have some time together."

He put the cruiser in gear and steered around the small cul-de-sac hotel entrance.

"It's not your fault. I'll still have this murder case to work on, not to mention keeping order among the children of love and brotherhood."

"They giving you fits?"

"Only moderately. Today was some kind of big Peace In or something. My uniformed men reported that they all sat on the ground in a big circle and chanted most of the day. It was almost harmonic sounding. The thing that's driving Mr. Mulvane to call us all the time is that there are just so *many* of them—more than a thousand at this point."

"So he's getting a taste of what his generosity has brought him."

"No good deed goes unpunished, you know." He turned onto Paseo del Pueblo and headed south.

Sam didn't have to wonder if that statement also pertained to volunteering for committees. She couldn't wait for this long ordeal to be over.

"You've been to Carinda's apartment," he said. "Let me know where to turn."

She spotted the turnoff about ten minutes later and directed him to the side of the building nearest Unit 6.

"I'll let the manager know what we're doing here," Beau said, scanning apartment numbers as they walked into the small courtyard. He handed Sam a set of keys, apparently from Carinda's purse.

Sam walked to Carinda's front door and unlocked it, pausing before going inside. Beau returned a couple minutes later and handed her a pair of latex gloves. The unit felt hollow and stale, despite the fact that its occupant had been here only yesterday morning. A trash can in the kitchen held packaging from a boxed microwavable breakfast— scrambled eggs and sausage—and the one dirty fork and orange juice-crusted drinking glass in the sink attested to the fact that this had probably been her last meal.

"The manager wants the place emptied by the end of the month. He's got someone from a waiting list ready to take it on the first," Beau said, glancing around at the cheap furnishings. "Doesn't seem like a lot of personal stuff here, does there?"

Sam truly looked at the place for the first time. Without Carinda's room-filling personality the place had the blandness of a two-star motel room. Commercial grade couch and armchair flanked a coffee table and end table of cheap material. The one lamp seemed like something that had come with the furnished apartment rather than an item Carinda would have chosen. A TV stand didn't even attempt to mimic the other wood laminates. A vanilla-scented candle stood in the center of the coffee table; that, and some DVDs under the new-looking television were the only touches the management probably had not provided. Not a single personal photo, no art or handmade pillows or throws.

"It really feels temporary, doesn't it?" she said.

"Yeah." He was busy rummaging through the contents of the shelf under the TV. "These movies are rentals. Goes along with your theory that she was only staying for the summer."

"Maybe she really only settled into the bedroom. I'll check."

The same generic furniture here—double bed with a plain headboard, one nightstand and a dresser that semi matched each other. The rumpled bedspread showed flashes of the sheets beneath, all of which looked like a bed-in-a-bag set that most likely came from Walmart. A discarded white sweater lay across the end of the bed and a pair of white sandals had been kicked off in the corner by the one window.

The dresser top contained a clutter of girly-stuff: a

puddle of silky lingerie which turned out to be three pairs of bikini panties with lace edging; a drinking glass held a clutch of makeup brushes, two with shades of blusher, two smaller ones with residue of the gold eye shadow Sam recognized as Carinda's shade. Plastic trays of the same blusher and eye shadow, three tubes of lipstick sprawled among the others. On the floor beside the dresser sat a half-full plastic laundry basket; in it Sam recognized the blouse Carinda had worn during the set-up phase of the festival.

Beau stood in the doorway.

"I haven't looked into the drawers yet," Sam said, pulling open the top one.

He told her he would take the bathroom while she worked the dresser.

Only two drawers held anything at all—more underwear and a few pairs of socks in the first one, three sweater twinsets and two folded tank tops in the second. The other two held dust balls that easily dated to the previous tenant. Sam moved on to the closet.

A dozen hangers held pants, blouses and one light jacket. Below them, on the floor, were walking shoes, black flats, and two pairs of heels that happened to go along with the colors of the clothing, which all fit the blue/yellow/orange color palette. Sam remembered that Carinda was wearing a blue dress when she died.

Also on the closet floor was a large, wheeled suitcase. Giving it a quick estimate, Sam would guess that all the clothing she'd come across so far would easily fit into it.

"It really looks like Carinda arrived in town with one suitcase of clothing and made a quick trip to Walmart to flesh out the décor of the apartment," Sam said when Beau emerged from the bathroom.

"It's pretty sparse in there, too," he said, holding up a zippered makeup bag similar to the one Sam used for her own things on short trips. "I'll ask the manager whether she signed a lease or had this place month-by-month."

"I haven't spotted a letter, an address book, or any type of personal memorabilia." Sam lifted the white sweater from the bed and started to fold it.

"Ah-so," Beau said in a Charlie Chan imitation. "What's this?"

In the folds of the bedspread, under the spot where the sweater had been, lay a cell phone.

"She didn't have the phone on her when she was found?" Sam asked.

He shook his head. "And there wasn't one in her purse. I guess I was so distracted that I failed to think beyond what was there, to consider what wasn't."

"Well, there's no landline in the apartment, so it makes sense that this is her only one."

He was already tapping buttons.

"Battery's almost dead. I may have to charge . . ." His voice trailed off. "Hmm. Recent calls. In the two days before she died there are six outgoing and two incoming. Four are local. Ha—one of them is to you."

Sam had talked to Carinda so many times during the planning and setup of the festival, she couldn't honestly remember who had called whom in those last couple of days.

"Here's one that I believe is a New York area code . . ." he tapped at the screen.

"Which fits with her driver's license. She would have been calling someone back home."

He listened intently for a minute then ended the call.

"It's a law firm. Hanover, Somebody and Somebody Else. I didn't catch all of it. Recorded message states their hours and Saturday evening at . . ." He glanced at his watch. "Nearly eight p.m. Eastern time is outside their work day. I'll have to call again on Monday."

He stared at the little screen. "Dang, battery just died. See if we can locate the charger for this thing, or I'll have to find a generic one."

Sam rummaged in the drawer of the nightstand—also remarkably sparse—and found what he needed.

"So, what do you suppose her story was?" she asked Beau after they had locked the apartment. "She bragged about who she knew as if she'd been here a long time."

He started the cruiser and backed out of the small space where he'd parked. "Wilson—the manager—says she paid a month at a time. When she rented the place she said she was waiting for her household things to arrive and had to have an apartment until she closed on the sale of her new place here."

"But we didn't find anything at all about a real estate purchase."

"No, we didn't. The one suitcase and rental car suggest that she never planned to be here all that long."

"It would fit with the remarks she made, about not putting up with all of us. She never really intended to stay."

"Odd though. Why join a committee and get so involved? It just doesn't fit with someone planning to move away quickly."

"Or with someone hiding out." Sam didn't know why that thought had popped into her head, but now that she'd said it she couldn't quite let go.

"What if she was? Hiding out, I mean. Getting away from someone back East. Maybe she was in trouble with the law there. It could explain why she had a lawyer."

"A reputable lawyer would recommend that she go back and turn herself in for whatever she was accused of. He would then be able to represent her in court and work to get her out of the jam."

"And when was the last time you had a suspect who would have done that? Especially if she was guilty?"

He tilted his head in acknowledgement. The Taoseño appeared on the right and he pulled into the restaurant's full parking lot. They stood in the vestibule for a few minutes until their turn came for a table. Sam ordered the chicken enchiladas—since Beau had earlier put that picture into her head—and he went for the burrito special.

"What other reasons could Carinda have had for joining the festival committee?" Sam mused after she'd taken a sip from her water glass. "Maybe there was someone in town she wanted to keep an eye on . . . one of the committee members or one of the vendors."

"Any idea which?"

"No, not at all. She didn't seem to form any friendships. If anything, it was the opposite. She managed to either tick them off or hurt their feelings. I chalked it up to her just being one of those people who isn't very good at social interaction."

"Well, Garcia didn't seem to come up with anyone who both hated Carinda and had the opportunity. Nearly everyone can be accounted for."

"Farrel O'Hearn and Danielle Ferguson were both away from the ballroom at the time of the murder."

"We called them in this morning," he said. "Apparently, they had a little row of their own. Questioned separately, they each gave nearly identical accounts, so I tend to believe that they alibi each other."

Sam pondered it all. She was missing some vital clue, almost certainly. No one really liked Carinda Carter, but she couldn't think of anyone with enough hatred to stab the woman. As Garcia had said, it took a lot of rage to do that. She finished her meal, then chided herself for not being more mindful of the amounts she was eating.

Beau pushed his own empty plate aside and reached over to take her hand.

"I don't know where you were just now," he said, "but don't worry about it. We will figure out what happened."

She gave him a thankful smile. It was nice to have someone else do the worrying. He drove back to the Bella Vista and pulled alongside her van in the parking lot.

"I won't stay at the bakery late," she promised. "A couple of hours to bake a torte and a few trays of cookies and brownies should do it. I can go back in the morning to ice them."

"If I can help you . . ."

The offer was generous but Sam knew she could finish more quickly on her own than if she had to stop and give instruction or help him find his way around the kitchen.

"You've had a long day already," she told him. "By the time you take care of the horses and feed the dogs, I'll probably be there."

She arrived at her shop, giving a quick look up and down the alley, half expecting to see Bobul again. No sign of him, of course. Inside, she switched on lights and turned on the oven, moving as automatically as she had in the early days before hired help, when she had to prepare enough baked goods in the pre-dawn hours to open the shop for the breakfast crowd. The routine was familiar and comforting; she found her mind wandering back over the events at the festival as she took eggs and butter from the fridge and measured flour and baking powder.

Friday morning, things had been crazy—no doubt about that. Most of the vendors had been busy with final setup, getting their product readied for sale. Since several of them were also committee members—herself and Harvey, especially—most of the organizational work had fallen to Rupert, Kelly and Carinda. Bentley Day had arrived at the hotel but had not yet shown up in the ballroom. Carinda had gone to search for him . . . Bentley's moves as told to Beau by the celebrity chef and the hotel bartender were somewhat different and Sam's own memory of the sequence of events was already becoming fuzzy.

She let the big mixer stir the brownie batter.

Several people had come looking for Carinda—Sam tried to remember who all they were. There had been a run-in between Farrel O'Hearn and Carinda, but Sam had considered it minor. Farrel's big competition was Danielle, so that was the battle that had stuck in Sam's mind. Of course, there was the fact that Farrel and Carinda had been wearing such similar dresses . . . Had she mentioned that to Beau, on the theory that Farrel might have been the real intended victim? She should say something to him when she got home.

Brownies into the oven, Sam started on the recipe for her Triple Chocolate Kahlua Torte.

Looking at this case from another angle, who had access to the murder knife? Early Friday morning, it had been with Bentley Day's props in that box under the judges' table. Carinda herself had shown it to Sam. And afterward? Carinda might have taken it from the box, thinking she should carry it upstairs to Bentley for when he made his grand entrance. A possibility.

What about the other vendors? The closest booths to the dais were Harvey's, Sam's, Farrel's and Susan Sanchez, one of the finalists in the contest. Of those, it kept coming back to Farrel as the one with the most grievance against Carinda. It would have been fairly simple for her to watch for a lull around the dais when no one else was present, stroll over there and duck behind the table for a moment. The knife wouldn't have been exactly inconspicuous, but many of the bakers had knives on the premises for slicing cakes. No one would have necessarily thought twice about someone carrying one around.

She poured the cake batter into round pans. The timer on the brownies showed only a few more minutes.

Of course, the fact that anyone could quietly carry a knife around, anywhere near the festival, pretty much opened the list of suspects right back up again. Face it— anyone could have done this.

Brownies came out of the oven, torte layers went in. They were thin enough to bake quickly, so Sam used the time to wash utensils. In the morning she could whip out a few batches of cookies and make frosting for the brownies and the torte. Being Sunday, she would have the place to herself.

The chair at her desk looked inviting—just for a few minutes to get off her feet—but exhaustion was setting in and it would be too easy to rest her head on her arms and end up sleeping there half the night. She kept moving.

At last the timer dinged for the torte layers. Ten more minutes before she could remove them from the pans, so she used that opportunity to organize space in the fridge for storage. When everything was neatly stashed away, she headed home.

Her eyelids felt heavy during the final few miles and she nearly missed the driveway turn. *I have to get some rest.* Pulling the van in beside Beau's personal SUV she got out and saw that the dogs were waiting for her on the porch. Her heart tugged a little—how nice that simple thing was, to be greeted with wags and excitement.

Nellie, the border collie, rubbed against Sam's legs when she stopped to give each of them some attention. Beau must have heard her vehicle; he opened the front door.

She stood up and started toward him, and that's when she smelled smoke. Faint and distant, but distinctly the smell of burning vegetation. She turned toward Beau.

"Yeah," he said. "The fire's still burning north of here. Wind's carrying the smoke right toward us."

Chapter 16

The bedcovers felt so good. Sam snuggled in closer to Beau, relishing the afterglow of predawn sex. They'd fallen into bed last night, both too tired for anything but a lazy goodnight. But somewhere around four, he reached for her and the timing was just right. Now, she wanted nothing more than to stay exactly where she was for the next two days.

That wouldn't happen, of course. The excitement of the chocolate festival was wearing off but the duty to be there had not yet gone away. One of her recommendations to the Chamber folks—if they planned to do this again—would be to make it a one-day event. Catch everyone at the peak of enthusiasm and end it while they still wanted more. Just her opinion.

There was also the real possibility there might not be

another festival at all. The murder was still making the news and more than once had been linked to the festival because of where it happened and Carinda's involvement with the committee. She drifted back to sleep almost hoping that the event would vanish for all time.

She woke to Beau's nudging.

"Sam? The alarm didn't go off. It's nearly seven," he whispered against her neck.

"Seven!" Almost a record sleep-in for her, these past two years. She sat upright, her heart pounding.

Spitting toothpaste into the sink, she forced herself to calm down. There wasn't that much yet to do at the bakery. She would be better off to think clearly and get the work done; even with cookies, brownies and a torte to finish she would still make it to the hotel by ten for the opening.

She walked into the ballroom at 9:57, in time to see Rupert put down the microphone after giving the usual morning pep rally and with enough time that she and Becky easily filled the display with the new items before people had drifted up to their booth. A glance around the room showed that most of the other vendors were present—only a few had completely given up the show, and for the most part the empty spaces had been put to good use with tables and chairs where folks could sit for awhile to enjoy coffee or tea with their dessert.

Despite the fact that Sam really just wanted this day to be over, she was glad to see that others were still on their toes to make it a quality event for the crowd. She and Becky did a brisk business in scones, muffins and coffeecake for awhile, then Kelly showed up.

"I never thought I would say this, but the smell of sugary things has no appeal at all for me today," she said to her mother. "What do you say to a real breakfast with eggs and bacon and everything? Right here in the restaurant—I'll buy."

Sam looked toward Becky, who said, "I had exactly that at home before I came. It did hit the spot—you guys go. I can handle things here."

An assessment of the room showed much thinner crowds than the previous two days. Becky could surely manage.

"Call me if you're swamped. I can come right back," Sam told her assistant.

A long buffet had been set up in the Bella Vista's restaurant, Sunday brunch in place of menu service. Sam filled a plate with protein and fruit.

"I really am reaching my saturation point with sweets and crowds and people in general," she said quietly to Kelly after they'd found a table beside a divider that partially screened it from the rest of the room. "Between the thousand and one hippies next door, the whole to-do over Carinda, and constantly having to smile while selling cheesecake slices . . . I'm ready for a break."

"Take one, Mom. You and Beau should book a trip and get away for awhile."

Sam laughed. "Well, a trip isn't going to happen. He's tied up with this case—who knows how long that will take—and I know he won't leave the ranch until the band of flower children go away. He's nervous as a bird about having that many of them around."

"How long will they stay?"

"Probably another month. Their leader said they have a big thing set up for summer solstice."

"No wonder Beau is antsy. At least you get to be done with *your* big-crowd event by the end of today."

Kelly glanced around the room, aware that others from the festival might be nearby. Sam peered over the divider.

"Speaking of Carinda . . .See that lady with her hair up in a clip?" Kelly asked. "Just leaving, bright turquoise top?"

Sam nodded, although she only caught a flash of the brilliantly colored shirt as the woman disappeared out the door.

"I saw her here the other day, too, kind of arguing with Carinda."

Who *didn't* argue with Carinda?

"It was something about money, is all I really got from it. They were standing in the alcove right by the ladies room and when I came around the corner they shut up really fast, like it was none of my business." She speared a strawberry and it dangled from her fork while she talked. "Which it wasn't. But it was funny to see the look on Carinda's face when she recognized me. I just ducked into the bathroom and ignored her. They were gone when I came out, but it was the last time I ever saw her—Carinda, I mean."

Thinking of seeing someone for the last time reminded Sam of Sarah Williams. She made a mental note to call the nephew after breakfast and find out what time the funeral would be.

"Good omelet, Mom. You should get one." Kelly had taken the time to have the buffet's chef make one fresh, while Sam had piled the pre-made scrambled eggs on her own plate.

"It looks good. But I'm getting full and I really should get back to Becky. Take your time to finish. I'll catch the tab up front."

"No, you don't. This was my treat."

Sam smiled at her daughter. It wasn't that long ago when Kelly had showed up after ten years away from home, jobless and in debt trouble. She'd done a great job of turning all that around.

"Okay, next time it's mine," Sam said.

Outside the restaurant she remembered to phone Marc Williams. He sounded busy, the sounds of voices in the background, but he told her that Sarah's funeral would be at two o'clock Tuesday. She stuffed her phone into her pocket and strolled slowly to the ballroom. No sign of the woman Kelly had tried to point out. If she spotted that turquoise blouse, Sam would try to speak to her. This would be someone else that Beau's men should question.

Booth sales seemed a bit slow, not only at the Sweet's Sweets location. Sam offered Becky a break if she wanted it.

"Nah, I'm fine. Today's hot item seems to be the torte you brought this morning. Not as much cheesecake."

It was always a guessing game, trying to figure out what to prepare the most of. At least cheesecake could go into the fridge and would last another day. Cookies and brownies were always welcomed at the homeless shelter and Sam could easily make a run by there at the end of the festival.

The next two hours dragged by. It was far easier to have the booth surrounded by impatient crowds and to be rushing around filling orders than to sit idly by and deal with a trickle of business. Sam signaled to Rupert when he stopped at Harvey's booth for ice cream.

"Do you suppose we could liven things up a bit?" she whispered to him. "Even Bentley Day yelling 'chop-chop' would be better than standing here twiddling our thumbs."

"Hang on to your hat, honey. Kelly scheduled a series

of radio spots that started at twelve. We want this thing to go out with a bang, so the raffle drawings are going to begin in another fifteen minutes. I'll space them out to keep people around until the judges make the big announcement at a quarter of two. When the prizes are announced, KVSN will be here to cover it live and a reporter and photographer from the *Gazette* are coming for it too."

"I truly did not mean to doubt you," she said, squeezing his arm. He seemed to have forgiven her for yesterday's law enforcement questioning.

Ask and you will receive, Sam thought as she looked up to see that the corridor outside the ballroom was already more crowded than just a few minutes ago.

Rupert picked up the microphone and gave a toss of his silver hair.

"Ladies and gentlemen . . . welcome to the final day of Sweet Somethings, the day when these five beautiful cakes now on display at the judges' table face the test of taste and beauty. Three prizes will be awarded, three of our fabulous bakers will go home with prize money and the acclaim of being winners in the First Sweet Somethings Chocolate Festival!"

Applause rose from the audience, even though only a handful had actually gravitated to the front of the dais at this point.

Sam couldn't believe she had walked right past the five finalists' cakes without really taking note of them; she nearly always checked out other bakers' creations. From her position in the booth, though, she could only see a yellow daisy sticking up from the top of one cake and a complicated-looking tangle of chocolate shapes on another. Just as she started to step out of the booth to take a look, four customers approached at once.

"Our judges will be announcing the winners in a little over an hour," Rupert continued. "For now, don't forget to come forward and take a good look at the five cakes then cast your ballot for the People's Choice Award. The cake with the most votes from our festival audience wins a special prize."

Sam wouldn't have minded competing for that one. In her quest for publicity for the festival, Kelly had convinced the local newspaper publisher to feature the People's Choice winner on the cover of their summer tourist magazine, along with a story about the winning baker. Sam couldn't have afforded to pay for that kind of advertising for Sweet's Sweets—the free publicity could have been invaluable. Alas, for appearance's sake, as head of the festival committee she had disqualified herself. Darn it.

Rupert picked up the fishbowl of ticket stubs and drew someone's name for a door prize. The throng continued to grow and Sam and Becky began madly bagging orders. She had no idea how much time had passed when she became aware that Bentley Day had taken over the MC duties.

"G'day, Taoseños!" he announced, giving away his New Mexico heritage by actually pronouncing the word correctly. "The time is here! We judges have made our decision. If you've not cast your ballot for the People's Choice, you have five minutes to bring it up here and put it in this." He held up a box which had been wrapped in *Qualitätsschokolade* logo paper.

Customers who had been scattered throughout the large room now began to migrate toward the dais, blocking access to others who were trying to get to the nearest booths.

"And now . . . what all of our contestants and all of our

visitors have been waiting for . . ." Bentley Day put on his biggest showman smile. "In third place—"

A man in front had been waving his arms wildly and now caught Bentley's attention.

"Vait!"

Sam could see his profile from where she stood—his stocky build, the round face with pink-apple cheeks, the cottony white hair. He wore a rather formal-looking three-piece suit and gold-rimmed eyeglasses. His right hand was in the air, index finger pointing toward the ceiling.

"Vait!" he said again. "Dis is not correct!"

Rupert and Bentley both leaned forward to hear him.

"You cannot avard the prize in this manner."

Rupert whispered, but unfortunately Bentley had not switched off the microphone so everyone in the large hall got every word.

"And you are?"

"I am Wilhelm Schott, president of *Qualitätsschokolade*. It is I who has given this prize!"

Everyone on the dais seemed momentarily stunned. Rupert looked toward Sam with *help* in his expression. She pushed through the crowd. At the very least she could insist he turn off the microphone until they solved the problem. She climbed the steps and took it from him.

"Folks, we will have this sorted out in a few minutes. Meanwhile, continue browsing and be sure to pick up those last minute gift items." She flicked the switch and set the microphone down.

"Mr. Schott, how nice to meet you. We are honored and so pleased that you could come to the festival."

The vivid blue eyes glared from under spiky white brows.

Sam took a breath. "Obviously, we missed something in your communication to us. I am—we all are—glad you came today so we can do this according to your wishes."

"One prize," he reiterated. "Goes to top baker only."

"Yes, yes. We will do that." She shot Rupert and Bentley a look that said *Work this out!* before she took Schott by the arm.

"While the judges evaluate their decision, let me treat you to a coffee," she said, leading him to the booth where she knew that Java Joe had created a superb brew using a hint of the sponsor's chocolate to make it the rave of the show.

Less than two minutes later, Rupert switched the mike on again. "All right! Sorry for that little delay. Since the judges had already made their first-place choice, that decision will stand." His eyes found Sam in the crowd and she nodded.

"All of our bakers have put enormous effort, many hours, and unbelievable creativity into their entries and now to honor them, we shall describe all five cakes before announcing our grand prize winner."

Sam's stomach settled a little; Mr. Schott seemed to be savoring his coffee. In the booth beside the coffee place, Danielle Ferguson was sending balls of imaginary hellfire toward Farrel O'Hearn.

"The first cake on our table," Rupert began, "is an elegant wedding cake from the kitchen of pastry chef Farrel O'Hearn. Each of the four dark chocolate cake tiers is shaped as a perfect globe, covered in shimmering ivory fondant. Tiers one and three are draped in swags of matching fondant, while the middle tier features hand-piped beaded frames around tiny cherubs. Between each tier are clusters of pink, coral and blush-rose gumpaste flowers.

This romantic cake is an absolute show-stopper."

A wave of applause for Farrel's cake.

"Is *schokolade*?" asked Mr. Schott. "I do not see it."

Sam ushered him to one of the tables where he could see the stage and yet relax with his coffee.

"Second in presentation is another wedding cake, this from local home baker Grace Maldonado. Square tiers of red velvet cake are draped in alternating white chocolate and dark chocolate fondant, smoothed to perfection. Cascading from the top, dark chocolate roses adorn the white chocolate tiers, while white roses offset the dark tier. The gorgeous flowers swirl around the cake and end in a trail of blossoms at the base. The black and white theme continues 'over the top' so to speak with a lush bouquet that any bride would love."

"Ah, now this one . . . she is *schokolade*." The Swiss visitor drained his cup and leaned back in his seat.

"Third on our table is a romantic pink confection from Susan Sanchez." Rupert moved to stand behind the cake in the center. "The dome-shaped chocolate mocha cake is covered in hundreds of delicate pink ruffle flowers made of molded white chocolate. Whether for a bride, a new mother, or your own little princess, this delicate creation will delight that special lady and all her guests."

The descriptions were beginning to sound like fashion show fare, and Sam spotted Rupert's writing flair in the narrative. Careful, she thought, someone's going to figure out your nom de plume.

"From the kitchen of Taos resident Cynthia Freeman," he continued, "comes this whimsical two-tier design of milk chocolate with dark chocolate chips in the cake itself. The rolled fondant decorations say Spring, with bright yellow daisies punctuating the chocolate and white stripes and a big yellow bow gives it an old-fashioned hatbox feel. On the top tier a sweet-faced honeybee rests his wings and we can only imagine that after his little nap he will be buzzing around the rest of the abundant yellow daisies in this beautiful little garden."

Cynthia must have brought family with her today; a cheer rose from one corner of the ballroom when Rupert finished describing the cake.

"Last, but most certainly not least," Rupert said, "we have Danielle Ferguson's entry, an all-chocolate wedding cake of four tiers. Each tall level of cocoa supreme cake is iced with chocolate ganache which is then covered in a smooth chocolate wall. Crisp chocolate 'lace' was molded to fit every surface of those walls, giving the overall effect of a delicate castle with ethereal parapets where the occasional white-chocolate flower peers out to the ordinary world below."

Sam had to hand it to him—he'd come up with more ways to describe chocolate cake than she would have ever imagined. And the contestants had displayed amazingly creative talent. She wondered if any of them was looking for a job—just in case Sweet's Sweets became even busier than at present.

Rupert handed the microphone to Bentley Day who, unable to be out of the limelight for more than a few minutes, had been providing boyish distractions at the back of the stage.

"Thank you for those lovely descriptions, Rupert. We have tallied the ballots that all of you, chocolate lovers of Taos, turned in, and I am pleased to announce that the winner of the People's Choice Award goes to . . . Cynthia Freeman for Honey Bee!"

Cheers erupted and applause came from all corners of the ballroom.

Cynthia blushed and slowly made her way from her booth at the very back of the room up to the front, where Bentley placed a ribbon with a medal around her neck. The photographer from the newspaper hustled forward for pictures. Apparently he suggested that the cake be moved to a separate area where he could set up the proper lighting because Cynthia picked it up and the little procession that included the reporter assigned to the story made their way, smiling and waving, out of the ballroom.

"Now, shall we find out who won the top prize?" Bentley Day teased the crowd.

No, let's just bag it and go home. What did he think? Sam tamped down her impatience for the day to be finished.

"In the judges' estimation," he began, "based on flavor of the cake, use of the *Qualitätsschokolade* product, and creativity of design . . . the top honor, and ten thousand dollar prize . . . goes to . . . Danielle Ferguson for her all-chocolate wedding cake!"

Next to Sam, Danielle shrieked and began to push through to the front. Farrel O'Hearn must have stepped aside for the cute little bee cake to pass by; she walked back into the ballroom at the moment Danielle's name was announced. Her face went stony, then red.

For a split second Sam thought she was seeing Carinda—Farrel's hair today fell in the same shape Carinda had always worn and her dress was the same blue color that the murdered woman had worn on her final day.

Danielle turned to her with a look of shock. She recovered quickly, however, and shot her rival a smile of smug triumph.

It was too much for Farrel, having the loss rubbed in her face that way. She lunged toward Danielle with a roar. The two women gripped forearms, snarling and clawing, pinwheeling out of control toward the table full of cakes.

Chapter 17

Several hundred people held their collective breath as the inevitable unfolded. Farrel's momentum propelled the two women directly toward the dais. The table holding the remaining four cakes teetered. The two female judges saw it coming and leaped to the very back of the platform just before the tallest of the cakes, Farrel's three-tiered creation of ivory fondant globes tilted forward and crashed onto her head. The wobbling table dispensed the other three cakes on top of the fighting women—splat! Cake, fondant, frosting and chocolate lacy bits shot out, covering a five-yard swath of the audience and nearby booths. Harvey Byron picked bits of cake out of his ice cream vats and in Sam's booth Becky and Kelly stared at each other in horror before they began to laugh at the sight of the pink and chocolate goo on their faces.

Sam turned to catch Herr Schott's reaction—dignified Swiss repulsion—right before he stomped out of the ballroom. Well. So much for any hope of another year's sponsorship.

As chair of the event she should probably be horrified at the battle between Danielle and Farrel, but the two women had been giving each other—and everyone else—grief since day one. The melee was almost inevitable. Danielle could have handled it better. A gracious winner is always more beloved than an arrogant one, and Danielle had been about as snotty toward Farrel as humanly possible. All in all, though, it really was pretty funny to watch the two of them rolling around in the wreckage of chocolate and icing on the floor.

Half the audience reacted similarly to the Swiss chocolate maker; a bunch of the others simply leaped in and began gobbling up hunks of broken cake and frosting flowers.

Auguste Handler showed up, alerted by shrieks from the room full of spectators and as soon as the two sugar-coated women were pulled apart he promptly presented them with a bill for cleanup. By this time all the other vendors were well into the process of breaking down their booths and hustling their belongings out the back door. It was more than an hour before Sam got away.

She pulled her van near the back door of the homeless shelter where she often donated spare baked goodies, hoping to give a lift in spirits to those who needed one. Her own mood had been strangely buoyed since the breakup of the fight that signaled the grand finale of the chocolate festival. Turning off her engine she walked to the back of the van to pull out three large bakery boxes filled with cookies, muffins, cake and cheesecake.

"Whoa, what's this? On a Sunday afternoon?" Greta Ortiz, who ran the shelter, greeted Sam at the door with a big smile and a hug.

Sam carried the boxes into the facility's kitchen and set them on the table.

"Mid-afternoon snack, dessert tonight, breakfast tomorrow . . . whatever you want it to be."

"I hear things got kind of exciting at the festival awhile ago," Greta said, taking a peek into the box on top.

"Uh-oh, this didn't get on the radio, did it?" Bad publicity, after all their hard work to make the festival a positive, upbeat event for the community?

"Oh, no. Nothing like that. In fact, the radio guy talked it up real big. The way your announcer described those cakes . . . made me want to run right down there and have some." Greta reached into the box, picked up a cookie and began nibbling the edges. "I got the skinny on the big fight from my gal who comes in to clean. Her sister was there and I'll tell you, she's no fan of Danielle Ferguson. She just had to call Sissy and pass along the word. Ooh, these chocolate cookies with all the nuts are really good!"

Including the word that Danielle had baked the winning entry? Sam closed her eyes for a moment and willed the whole scene out of her head. She was bone tired and ready to be done with everyone associated with the festival.

For now. She was sure to keep hearing about Carinda's murder and had a sneaking suspicion that someone involved with the festival would end up being implicated. She could only hope that, if it was Bentley Day or one of the other out-of-towners, Beau was close to figuring it out and making an arrest.

As Sam was leaving, Greta thanked her profusely and assured her that the people they fed for the next couple of days would love the extra treats. Sam started her van and dialed Beau.

"If you don't have any objection," she said, "I'm picking up deli food for dinner. Roast chicken, salads and rolls okay with you? I can't seem to summon up the energy to cook."

"I'll go you one better. I'm about a block from the store now—I'll even pick up the food."

Well, what woman in her right mind would say no to an offer like that? She headed north on Paseo, cruising slowly along. The midday temperature hovered around eighty, with a crystalline blue sky and a sharp quality to the light. She realized what a perfect weekend she'd nearly missed, stuck indoors for most of three days.

Passing the municipal complex she glanced that direction just in time to catch a flash of turquoise clothing. A blonde woman with her hair up in a clip, hands cuffed behind her back, was being led into the building by a uniformed officer. Her appearance so closely fit what Kelly had described at breakfast that Sam whipped her steering wheel to the right and bounced a little as the van took the driveway a bit too fast.

Beside the city patrol car at the curb stood another officer; Sam recognized him as she pulled in closer.

Ray Hernandez looked up from his clipboard. "Sam, hi. Um, you always this eager to visit us?"

"Sorry about that little screech of tires." She put her gearshift in Park and killed the engine. "Who's that woman that was just being taken in? Does this have anything to do with one of Beau's cases?"

A wrinkle of puzzlement flicked across his brow.

"Don't think so," he said. "We had a 10-14 call, prowler alert. Caught her breaking and entering. Why? You know her?"

Sam shook her head. "Not personally. But she was seen this morning near the scene of another crime."

"Let me guess—the murder that the sheriff is working on?"

"Yeah. What's her name?"

"Kaycee Archer, according to her ID. We caught her, apparently, just after she got the screen off a back window of someone's place and was trying to force the glass open. She didn't actually steal anything. She won't be here long— seems to have plenty of money so she'll post her own bond right away."

Hernandez seemed eager to get inside so Sam started her van again and pulled away, pondering what he'd just told her. Why did that name sound familiar? She had heard it somewhere and the fact that Kaycee had been at the hotel this morning . . . she had to be connected with someone at the festival. The   question was, who?

Sam found her attention wandering. It had been a tiring weekend, with a long and strenuous week leading up to it. She could feel the adrenaline draining out of her. All she wanted to do now was get home, kick off her shoes and spend a quiet evening with Beau.

* * *

Monday morning he rose early and managed to do the ranch chores and leave for work without waking her. When she came downstairs she found a note propped against her favorite coffee mug—"Hope you slept well"—followed by a scrawled outline of a heart.

She filled her mug from the carafe he'd so thoughtfully made for her, telling herself that she would take the morning off and just roam around the house in her robe and slippers. But once she'd drunk the first dose of caffeine she felt too wired to sit around. A shower, a fresh baker's jacket, and she walked in the door at Sweet's Sweets a little after nine o'clock.

"Hey, what happened to your idea of taking the whole day off?" Becky asked, standing near the worktable with her own coffee cup in hand.

"Couldn't do it. Sleeping until seven-thirty *is* late for me. It already feels like I've taken half the day off."

Jen stepped through the curtain from the sales room, hearing Sam's voice. "Things are pretty quiet here. Maybe everyone in town got their pastry fixes over the weekend."

"That's fine," Sam said. "We can all use a breather. We're getting into the wedding season and pretty soon we'll be looking back fondly on this day."

Becky set her cup down and returned to a beach-themed birthday cake. Sam sat at her desk, knowing she would have a zillion emails and figuring she'd better take inventory of all her supplies to be sure they could handle an influx of large cakes during the coming weeks. Before she'd finished her list, Jen buzzed her on the intercom to announce that Beau was on the shop's phone.

"Hey there," he said. "I didn't want to call your cell and wake you up. In case you really had managed to stay home for a restful day. Looks like I know you pretty well."

She laughed. "That you do."

"I reached that lawyer in New York," he said.

Lawyer? Her mind went blank.

"The number we found on Carinda Carter's phone. Charles Hanover of Hanover, Ruskin and Hanover. I told him we were trying to locate Carinda's next of kin."

"Oh! Yeah, what did he say?"

"He said he would notify them. Otherwise, he wouldn't discuss it much, even when I said that I was investigating her murder. Playing the attorney-client privilege card unless I come up with a court order for further information."

"So, nothing?"

"All he would tell me was that Carinda had told him she was getting away for awhile, pending the outcome of a court case."

"What kind of case?"

"He wouldn't even tell me that. The guy was pretty rude. Treated me like a rube lawman from the sticks."

"So . . ."

"So, I'll get that court order and we'll proceed from there. If this court case he mentioned has any bearing on Carinda's death the prosecutor will, no doubt, hammer him for any scrap of admissible evidence. Of course, first we have to have a suspect and make an arrest."

It sounded like a merry-go-round of gamesmanship in the legal system.

"Curious. I wonder what Carinda was running from. Maybe there's an ex-husband or abusive boyfriend in the picture somewhere."

"There could be, and that might be what the whole court thing is about, although I'm not sure why the attorney wouldn't tell me so. I'm just now catching people in their offices where I can start asking questions about the lady and her past life. According to her Social Security records, her last employment was with a graphic arts firm in New Jersey. I've got a call in for the head of the department to see if I can find out more about why she left."

Sam heard his intercom line ring in the background.

"Sorry, darlin'," he said after a short pause. "It's Ray Hernandez. I'd called him earlier about that10-14 you told me about yesterday. Maybe he's got answers for us."

Last night over their dinner of roast chicken Sam had mused aloud about Kaycee Archer and the fact that Kelly had overheard her arguing with Carinda before her death. Beau had promised to get more details about Kaycee's arrest.

As she entered her supply order, Sam found herself thinking about Carinda and wondering why none of them knew much about the woman's life before she'd arrived in Taos. For someone who constantly wanted to be in the middle of things she had talked very little about her past. Sam decided she should call a final meeting of the festival committee, along with some of the Chamber board members, as a debriefing on the event and to decide if there would be another one next year. Maybe she could ferret out personal info on Carinda from someone who'd known her better.

She got so caught up with that subject that she nearly ordered five pounds of sugar instead of the fifty she needed. Shoving aside thoughts of festival business for the next hour, she concentrated on her own work.

When Beau stopped by to see if she was interested in lunch she looked around, feeling a bit like a groundhog emerging into the light. Julio's area of the kitchen was clean and well organized and he said he was making a batch of their basic muffin ingredients for the following day; Becky had finished the adorable beach scene cake, complete with brown sugar sand and sugar-paste umbrellas. They assured Sam the shop could spare her for awhile.

Outside, the day had turned much warmer and the wind had increased, kicking up little dust devils in the school ground a block away and sending tan ribbons of dirt skittering down the streets.

Beau backed his cruiser out of its parking space and headed south. "I still haven't done a thorough search of Carinda's place and I think it's high time I do that. That New York lawyer might try to withhold information from me, but there have to be things I can learn right here in town."

"Want some help?"

"Sure—let's grab something to eat before we tackle it."

Since she'd only eaten a blueberry muffin this morning and it was already nearing two p.m., Sam didn't argue with that logic. They went through the Taco Bell drive-up and carried their bag of tacos to the apartment. Eating the fast-food lunch at Carinda's small kitchen table felt a little weird, but Sam was still mulling the information from the attorney.

"If Carinda left New York because of a boyfriend or husband, I suppose he would be a logical suspect, someone with the rage to stab her. He could have tracked her here, no matter how careful she thought she was being," Sam said, taking a swig of her soft drink. "Maybe we'll find some kind of written record, some evidence of a philandering boyfriend or her own medical records proving someone had abused her."

"For all we know, the attorney himself might have advised her to get away from New York and hide out in a

place none of her old contacts would think to look. I just
don't get why he wouldn't have told me that."

He looked around the bare-bones room. "And if her
killer was one of our other suspects—Bentley Day or Farrel
O'Hearn—maybe we'll find evidence to cinch the case. My
forensic team is still checking records from the cell phone.
You'd be amazed what people will say in a text message, like
they have no clue those records can be accessed later."

Sam glanced from the small kitchen to the living room.
"Where do you suggest we start?"

"We didn't give much attention to the kitchen the other
day," he said, wadding up the last of his paper wrappers.
"Why don't you start here? Be sure to look inside places
like canisters and food storage bowls, and also check the
undersides of drawers and shelves. I'll take the bedroom,
even though we pretty much went through that already.
Maybe there's something we missed."

Sam left the empty food bag on the table so they could
take it with them. She was vaguely aware of Beau leaving
the room as she opened the first set of cupboard doors and
began taking out dishes. She set some cheap earthenware
plates aside and had started opening the lids on plastic
bowls when she heard Beau's phone ring in the other room.
Before she'd gone through the first section of cabinet he
rushed into the room.

"I gotta go." His face was pale, his voice tight.

"What's the matter? You feel okay—?"

"It's the peace-and-love bunch. They made a big
bonfire, which went out of control and got into some old
crop stubble. It's spreading. Right toward our place."

Chapter 18

Sam felt her heart thud. She dropped a blue plastic bowl and started toward him.

"You don't need to come," he said. "I've got dispatch calling the Forest Service to organize resources to fight it. Main thing is that I'll need to get the horses into their trailer and out of there. Rodriguez has the same problem so we'll help each other." Beau was already at the door, a hand on the knob.

"But, shouldn't I—?"

"Right now, extra people and vehicles are just going to get in the way. Already, Rico says he chased some guy off our property, thinking he might be a looter." He noticed her expression. "Darlin', please—I don't want to hurt your feelings. But really—it's better that you aren't there. Just stay here and keep searching for what we talked about. Helping me solve this murder case is every bit as important as anything else you could be doing at home at the moment."

He was out the door before she could formulate an argument.

She turned back to the cupboard, glancing at the underside of each dinner plate as she put it away, unable to stop thinking of a field of flames being whipped by the wind toward their property. The wooden barn, the horses and dogs, their own fields of new corn and alfalfa, barely out of the ground this early in the season. The log house. Her tacos threatened to come up and she ran for the bathroom.

False alarm, except that she found herself breathing hard and struggling not to imagine the worst.

Get a grip, Sam. Get those pictures out of your head and go back to work. Find the evidence, then you can call Kelly to come pick you up. She walked to the bedroom. It made more sense that Carinda would have hidden things there than in the kitchen anyway. She saw that Beau had opened the closet and put Carinda's suitcase on the bed. His phone call must have come just as he was about to open it.

The bag had a long zipper that ran around three sides of it, along with others that opened two smaller sections on top. She pulled at the long one and lifted the lid. Inside, the bag looked completely empty. As she swung the lid of the suitcase fully open, she noticed that it seemed heavy for its size. Taking another look at the zippered sections, one of them contained a sheaf of papers. She reached in and pulled out the whole batch, allowing herself a little mental *ah-ha!* moment.

Travel brochures lay on top of the pile, which contained documents of some sort, a large brown envelope addressed to Carinda Carter at a New York City address, a cluster of newspaper clippings, and a business-sized envelope addressed to Carinda here in Taos. Sam sat on the bed and spread out the cache of information.

The business-sized envelope was from the law firm in New York, the same one Beau had called. Inside, a single-sheet letter from Charles Hanover informed Carinda of a court date in early July that she would need to attend. The larger envelope contained a thick bunch of pages— two stacks of stapled sheets with a legal-looking blue cover sheet on each. A quick peek at the top page: Last Will and Testament of Julia A. Joffrey.

Why did that name seem so familiar? Sam closed her eyes for a moment and saw it in print. That copy of *People* magazine with the article about the wealthy heiress who had died a few months ago, leaving her family embroiled in a big battle.

Farrel O'Hearn, in her booth at the festival, had been telling someone that she 'knew the old bat.' Finally, the connection Sam had been seeking between Farrel and Carinda. Her gaze fell to the little clutch of news clippings. The longest one carried the headline: Heiress's Estate Remains a Muddled Mess. Sam picked it up and began skimming the lines.

Joffrey had inherited a fortune from her father's lucky entry into the airline business at the moment when air travel was coming into its own in the mid-twentieth century. Instead of operating an airline himself, Randal Joffrey had started supplemental businesses that would prove crucial to the industry—fuel, food service, even the manufacture of airsick bags and those ubiquitous yellow life jackets. But where he had really amassed the fortune was in spotting those cities that would eventually become hubs for major airlines and buying up cheap country property all around their existing tiny airports. When Randal died in 1982 at the relatively young age of sixty-four, his will was quite clear—his daughter Julia inherited it all, an estimated fifty billion dollars at the time. Julia's mother had died some twenty years earlier than Randal, and he made it clear that neither his second or third wives, nor any of their offspring, would get a cent.

The problem arose when Julia never married and never had children of her own. The line of succession for the vast fortune was unclear by law, and as she aged Julia tended to go with her whim of the moment, which had always been her way—according to 'unnamed sources' in the news article. She had rewritten her will at various stages of her life leaving the massive fortune—at different times—to her half-siblings (in defiance of Daddy's wishes), to a nurse who had cared for her when she became permanently crippled at the age of fifty, to an art museum, and to her dogs.

According to the articles, the last known will left measly one-million-dollar bequests to the nurse and the dogs, with all the rest of it going to a favorite half-niece—Carinda Carter.

Sam felt the breath go out of her. She looked around. What on earth was a billionairess doing living in this dump of an apartment? Then it dawned on her; this is what the big court case was about. The will was surely being contested and Carinda had not actually received her inheritance yet. Sam dropped the news articles and picked up one of the copies of the will.

She ran her finger down the lines of type, skimming, hoping to find the bottom line. The language was obscure legalese and it was no wonder the lawyers were having a field day racking up billable hours while they sorted it out. Buried in the middle of the ream of paper, one provision caught her eye. If she was reading it correctly it looked as if, in the event Carinda died before she inherited, the whole thing would be meticulously divided among that throng of Julia's half-siblings, their children and grandchildren, and a variety of charitable causes. What a mess. What a motive!

Even if hundreds of other people came into the picture, the money was so astounding that any one (or all of them in cahoots) would end up better off than the Powerball lottery winners from all time. No wonder Carinda had chosen to hide out, probably on advice of her lawyer. But there was that court date in July. She had to stay alive long enough to get there and to receive the inheritance. Once hers, she could write her own will and do with the money as she wished.

Oh, Carinda, there were so many other ways you could have played this. Assume another name during the hiding time, get your lawyer to work through two or three intermediaries, and for god's sake, stay low-key! Sam shook her head. When it came right down to it, Carinda's pushy ways and noisy arguments might have very well been the thing that got her noticed. Anyone who was following the whole Joffrey fiasco in the media might have inadvertently pointed the finger right at Carinda. Sam almost felt sorry for the poor little wealthy girl.

She turned to the last page of the will, wondering if it included a listing of those snubbed relatives when she heard a sound. Beau had probably come back. She stepped into the living room doorway. A woman stood just inside the apartment, looking around, getting her bearings.

Tall, blonde hair to her shoulders, flawless complexion

with shapely pink lips, form-fitting designer jeans and a red, short sleeved cashmere sweater. She carried a large brown envelope and had a tiny purse dangling from her shoulder. The expensive hair and manicure—Sam realized it was Kaycee Archer.

Little things began to fall into place: the visits where Kaycee was looking for Carinda, the argument Kelly had overheard at the hotel, the police arresting Kaycee for trying to break into this apartment.

Kaycee started visibly when she saw Sam, her pale face going a little whiter.

"What are you *doing* in my sister's apartment?" she demanded.

"I'm here on Sheriff's Department business, investigating a murder. So I'll ask you the same question—what are *you* doing here?"

"I saw the sheriff drive away. And you're no official person, not in that baker's uniform."

"Fine. I'll be happy to call the sheriff and get him right back here. I think he's going to believe my story more than yours. You still didn't answer my question. Carinda's *sister*? Really?"

Kaycee's eyes went to the sheaf of papers in Sam's hand.

"We have a complicated family but, yes, we're as close as sisters. I need those documents," she announced, taking a step toward Sam.

"Unh-uh. The sheriff is going to turn them over to the court and the legal system can figure it all out."

The shapely pink mouth went into a straight line and the deep brown eyes turned glittering black. "No way. They've dicked around with this long enough."

"Are you acting on your own or are all the half-siblings

and cousins twice-removed in on this too?" Sam asked, playing for time while her mind scrambled madly to figure out what to do. Kaycee was a good four inches taller, although Sam could certainly take her in the bulk-and-muscle department. Her phone was lying beside the pile of news clippings on the bed—a lot of good that would do her—if she couldn't persuade the woman to leave, there wasn't a single weapon in reach.

"Give me the documents," Kaycee repeated. She took a step forward.

"Let me get this straight—Julia's will states that Carinda receives the entire estate, but if Carinda died before receiving the inheritance it gets split a lot of ways." It dawned on Sam that it was definitely in Kaycee's best interest to kill her half-sister.

Kaycee's face hardened another degree. She was becoming less attractive by the moment.

"Did you—?" She couldn't bring herself to level a direct accusation. "Why on earth would you hang around town? I mean, wouldn't you want to put a lot of distance between you and Taos, and get somebody to swear you'd never set foot here."

"It wasn't like that. I had to talk to her."

"Ah, yes, a talk that turned into an argument. It was overheard by quite a few people." Surely a lie doesn't count when it's a murderer you're lying to. "And the argument somehow got taken outside and . . . when did the knife come into it? You pick it up on your way through the ballroom and just brazenly carry it out to the garden?"

"I don't know what you're talking about and I certainly never held a knife on anyone."

Sam was working to figure out what parts of that

statement might be true when the front door suddenly opened.

"Kaycee, what's taking so—?" Harvey Byron jolted to a halt in the doorway, his stare taking in the whole scene.

Sam's mind whirled. Two against one in the garden . . . But Harvey? Mr. Nice Guy couldn't possibly figure into this.

Harvey gave Sam a long look then took a step back. "I don't know anything about this, Sam." He tried for a sincere expression as he spoke.

"Harvey! Help me out here. She's got the real will." Kaycee's eyes went a little wild now that she wasn't so sure of her backup. Her teeth clenched as she spoke again. "Harvey, the *money*. This is for *us*, for your dream."

Sam had a flash vision of running into the bedroom and snatching up her phone while their attention was on each other. Beau was too far away to get to her but maybe the police . . . She edged one step away. Harvey saw her.

"C'mon, Samantha," he said, opting for persuasion—for now. He gave that shy smile and nodded toward the pages in her hand. "Let's just have a look."

And once this will is out of my hands—what then? Surely the envelope Kaycee had brought contained some other document, something that would name her the sole beneficiary, and no doubt she had messed with the dates, signatures or something else so that her version might actually supersede the other one. Harvey took two steps slowly toward Sam, raw greed now showing behind his normally quiet façade.

"See, Sam, we have plans for this money," Kaycee pleaded. "We'll get married and run Harvey's ice cream shop empire tog—"

"Kaycee, dear," he interrupted without taking his eyes

off Sam. "Please stop talking. Please wait outside."

He turned to look at his lover and in that fraction of a second Sam spun around and made a dash for the bedroom. She slammed the door behind her, struggling to twist the flimsy doorknob lock.

With a roar, Kaycee charged and the insubstantial hollow-core door shuddered inward dangerously. Another body slam. Surely the pounding now included both of them. Sam flew to the bed and grabbed up her phone, needing three tries with shaking hands to get through to 911.

"Hurry! There are two of them, right outside the bedroom door!"

"Stay on the line, ma'am," said the automaton voice that was supposed to be calm and reassuring but only had the effect of making her want to scream. "I'm dispatching officers to your location now."

The door shook again, the wooden doorjamb giving a loud *crack!*

"Please tell them to hurry!" Sam said. "They've already killed one woman."

Talking to the dispatcher wasn't accomplishing anything, she realized. She set the phone on the dresser and scrambled to gather the papers she had left strewn on the bed. Legal documents, news clippings, envelopes—she whisked them into a messy pile and picked them up. *What to do? Get them out of sight—at least make Harvey's job that much harder.* She hugged the papers to her chest and scurried back to the dresser. Sliding open the third drawer she dumped it all inside and pushed it closed just as the door frame splintered, the door banging open against the wall, Harvey falling into the bedroom.

Sam snatched up her phone, caught the dispatcher's

voice asking if she was still on the line.

"Yes, I'm here! He's broken into the room—I'm cornered!"

Harvey jumped to his feet and came toward her. Behind him, Kaycee stood with her brown envelope hugged to her chest, making little mewling sounds and seeming a little shocked by his violent approach. He took another ominous step.

"Where's the damn will?" he demanded.

Sam forced her eyes away from the dresser, flicking a quick look at the open suitcase. He took the bait, picking up the bag and shaking it in hopes something would drop out.

At the moment he figured out the case was empty, Sam heard the reassuring sound of sirens in the parking lot beyond the bedroom window. She stiffened. This was the make-or-break moment.

Fortunately, Kaycee broke first and Harvey turned to look at her for the first time.

"We have to get out!" she screamed with a wild look in her eye.

Harvey gave it thoughtful consideration for about two seconds. He shot Sam a malevolent look and then rushed out after Kaycee.

Sam's breath went out in a whoosh.

At the apartment's front door she heard voices.

"Whoa, whoa, whoa," said a male. "Nobody's going anywhere."

She slipped out of the bedroom and saw that two Taos Police officers were blocking the open doorway. Kaycee's shoulders were shaking as Ray Hernandez lifted the brown envelope out of her hands.

"Ms. Kaycee Archer. Twice in twenty-four hours . . . you must really like our facilities. Well, you know the drill." He placed a hand on her shoulder and turned her around.

The other officer stepped forward and snapped handcuffs on her.

All the bluster seemed to have gone out of Harvey Byron, as well. He made a half-hearted attempt to back away from the police but there was really nowhere in the small apartment to hide and no back escape route. He submitted to being cuffed and by the time they'd led him out to the narrow walkway in front of the apartments, he was already turning on the charm, trying to make it sound as if he'd come along to break up an argument between the two women.

"Sam, you okay?" Officer Hernandez asked.

She nodded although her heart hadn't actually slowed down much yet.

"Look, I don't know if it's anything or not, but I heard some stuff on the scanner about Beau. You can come with me and we'll radio."

Beau? An icicle formed in her gut.

Chapter 19

S am, I'm sure he's fine. Take a deep breath, get your
things, and I'll give you a ride," Hernandez said.

She stumbled back to the bedroom, a fog of unreality
around her head. Phone. Her backpack. The evidence. Beau
would want the evidence.

She opened the dresser drawer and stuffed the various
papers and clippings into the largest of the envelopes, then
jammed the whole mess into her pack.

Out in the parking lot the first car was rolling with
Kaycee and Harvey in the back seat behind the metal screen
that separated them from the officer. Ray Hernandez was in
the driver's seat of the other, the passenger door standing
open for her. Sam slid in gratefully.

"I need to—" she began, but Ray had already picked up
his mike, speaking in low tones. "Here you go, Sam. Sheriff

Cardwell's on this frequency."

"Beau?" she felt her voice crack a little.

"Sam, I'm fine. We're on a public frequency so I have to keep this short." Meaning, watch what you say. She could hear helicopters in the background. "The fire has spread. I have to tell you that we're evacuating homes to the south and west of the Mulvane property. That includes us, so you can't come home. I'm here now, and I can grab valuables, whatever I can fit into my cruiser."

The news barely skimmed the edge of her consciousness. Evacuate. That meant the house could very well burn to the ground. Valuables—how did one decide?

She looked down at her left hand; her wedding band and his mother's garnet ring were safe.

"I've taken the horses to another ranch, out of the danger zone," he was saying, "and the dogs are already in the cruiser."

Her thoughts went to the carved wooden box, the one irreplaceable artifact she'd ever owned in her life. She didn't want to mention it over the radio.

"My jewelry box— Is your safe fireproof?" she asked. She couldn't honestly remember whether she'd put the box back in there or left it in its usual spot on the bathroom vanity, but she hoped he would pick up the clue.

"It is," he said, "but I'll retrieve your things. All the photos are on the computer, right? I've got that already. Wait for me at your shop or at Kelly's or at my office."

Thank you. Thank you for being the guy I can rely on to think of everything.

"Beau? Stay safe. There's nothing in that house worth losing you."

He broke radio protocol by saying that he loved her,

then she heard him cough and realized the smoke must be terrible. She handed the mike back to Hernandez and blinked to conceal the tears that pooled now in her eyes.

As much as Sam wanted to listen in on the questioning of Kaycee Archer and Harvey Byron, she knew she couldn't focus enough to make sense of it. Beau would have his turn at them later anyway. She said as much to Ray Hernandez as he followed the other cruiser toward the police station.

"If you can drop me off at my bakery, I'll get my own vehicle," she said.

It seemed a lifetime ago since Beau had come by to get her and they had picked up tacos for lunch. In reality, when she walked into the Sweet's Sweets kitchen, it wasn't even quitting time yet.

"Sam, are you okay?" Becky said, dropping her pastry bag on the worktable. "You look like you were mugged by a ghost or something."

Julio stared at her, nodding. "Pretty white in the face."

She stepped into their small restroom and looked in the mirror. Her hair stuck out at odd angles—probably because she'd repeatedly run her fingers through it during the radio conversation with Beau—and she had to admit that every scrap of blusher and lipstick she'd applied that morning was gone.

Becky peered around the edge of the open door. "We heard about the fire. You can smell the smoke all over town."

Sam nodded. The haze and odor of woodsmoke had lingered so many days now that she'd become used to it.

"It's out there near your place, isn't it?"

Her head bobbed but she refused to think about what might be going on at the moment.

"The radio says they have tanker planes and helicopters

on it. I'm sure the houses will be safe." Becky squeezed Sam's hand as she said it.

Sam nodded again, squared her shoulders and walked back into the kitchen, staring at her desk as if she didn't quite know what to do next. No matter how much she coached herself, she could not get rid of an image of their beautiful log home in flames.

"Sam? Earth to Sam . . ." Becky had apparently tried to get her attention more than once. "Look, you're exhausted and this whole fire situation isn't helping."

And she didn't even know about the confrontation only a little while ago over the vast Joffrey fortune.

"Why don't I call Kelly next door and she can take you to her place. Get some sleep. You'll hear from Beau soon, I know you will."

"I can go over there by myself," Sam insisted. "I'll pop in and tell her what I'm doing but there's no point in interrupting her work day."

She put on as bright a smile as she could manage.

Out in the alley, she paused near her van. She could go to Kelly's—to the home she'd lived in nearly thirty years before meeting Beau—but she knew she would never sleep. There was no point in pacing through the rooms or, worse yet, raiding the fridge of all the snack foods she knew Kelly kept on hand. She stared at the hazy sky for several minutes before getting into the vehicle.

It seemed to steer itself through the streets, covering the few blocks to Beau's office. The one place where she would receive up-to-date news about the fire situation and the most likely place Beau would come first when his duties were done. She found a street-side parking spot and fed the meter all the change she could dig up.

The deputies in the squad room greeted her in much the same way her own crew had—with the kind of sympathy that only served to make her worry. At least, they informed her, no homes had yet succumbed to the fire.

"I'd like to hang out in Beau's office if that's okay," she said to Rico. "To wait until he comes in."

The deputy nodded and stepped aside for her. "I'll tap on the door if there's any news. If you feel like you want to stretch out awhile, the cell is empty right now."

She smiled at his kindness but was too tired to be cheerful.

Behind Beau's solid door she set her pack on his desk and started pulling things out. The legal documents and news clippings she'd brought from Carinda's apartment had become wrinkled and she occupied her mind by smoothing and putting them into some sort of order that Beau could comprehend when he got back to working the case.

She pulled out her phone, surprised it hadn't been ringing constantly as friends began hearing the news of the fire. Anyone who knew the area would easily figure out that the blaze was very near their home, and it would only be standard country courtesy for people to offer to help with evacuation or to give them a place to sleep. When she pressed the power button she discovered why—her battery power was in the red zone. She rummaged a little further and came up with the charger cord and plugged it in.

Within minutes it rang and she discovered there were fifteen voicemail messages.

"Mom! Where have you been?" Kelly's voice held a frantic edge.

You wouldn't believe. "My battery went dead and I didn't realize it."

"I was so worried—they're saying the fire is close to some ranch houses."

"Beau's handling it. I don't know any more than that."

"But you're safe?"

"We are. Look, I've had messages from nearly everyone. I guess I better start calling them back."

The situation lost impact with each retelling and by the time Sam had recounted her afternoon to Rupert, Zoë, Jen and Becky she felt less traumatized; now she was just plain tired. She leaned forward in Beau's chair and put her head on his desk for a minute. Somehow the minute must have turned into a couple of hours; a sound grabbed her attention and she raised her head.

Beau moved with the slowness of exhaustion, but something in the set of his face told her that everything was probably all right. The smell of smoke wafted off his clothing and when he removed his Stetson, it was easy to see the grime on his face. She smiled at the sight of him.

"Hey, baby," she said, rising to stroke the side of his face.

He pulled her close but a couple of deep breaths later she coughed and had to retreat to arm's length.

"How is it?"

"Fire's well under control. Didn't get any structures on our place, but I was worried for the barn. For awhile there, the wind was carrying the leading edge of the flames straight toward it. Close to sundown it shifted and the tanker was able to drop enough slurry to douse it. Our new corn is gone and I doubt the west alfalfa field will come back. We'll see."

"Do you have Ranger and Nellie with you?"

"Kelly has them. I went by your shop first and when

she came out she offered to take them in to Riki's place and give them baths. Said she would take them home with her tonight and bring them back in the morning. You wouldn't believe how smoky they smelled."

Sam gave him a long gaze and laughed.

"Uh, yeah, me too, I guess."

"What about damage at the neighbors?"

"Max Rodriguez's place is all right—he was upwind. Mulvane's lost his barn and two sheds. His crops are pretty well wiped out, but that's more because of vehicles and trampling than the fire. Pisses me off the way these 'love the earth' types often do such stupid things in the name of protecting it. Don't get me started."

"Won't they have to pay for the damage?"

"Yeah, well, all I could do was issue citations for having unlawful clearances around their campfires. There'll be fines, and I'm sure Mulvane will try to make them pay for his lost buildings. That Moondoggie was stomping around, whining about how there's fire retardant all over their buses. I'll be real surprised if he actually comes to the courthouse and pays the fines."

"So they haven't left?"

He shook his head. "We took them away from the campsite during the operations, for their safety, but they went right back as soon as the area was cleared."

He glanced through some message slips on his desk and picked up the envelope Sam had left there.

"That's evidence for your murder case," she said, belatedly remembering her own close call during the afternoon. "Kaycee Archer and Harvey Byron showed up together. I think they were vying against Carinda for the huge Julia Joffrey estate. Taos PD has them both in custody now."

"Sam . . . did you put yourself in danger to get this?"

She waggled her hand back and forth. "Not too much."

His ocean blue eyes held her gaze firmly.

"Well, maybe a little. I'd found the documents and was about ready to get out of the apartment when they came walking in. Things are starting to make sense, though. Kaycee kept trying to find Carinda before the festival started, then there were a few times I spotted Harvey and Kaycee talking. Silly me, I thought he had some kind of new romance going on. Maybe that's part of it." She stood up. "Oh—not to mention that Harvey would have had easy access to that knife. His booth was very near the dais."

"Okay. I guess that'll be my job tomorrow, questioning the two of them. Unless they gave confessions when the cops showed up?"

"Unfortunately, no. By the time you get there, I wouldn't be surprised if they turn on each other. Harvey sure wanted that money. I don't know who charmed who or what started the two of them working together, but I doubt he's willing to let Kaycee send him to prison over it."

He reached for her hand. "I'm just glad you're safe. Let's go home."

The night air felt clear and cool after the heat and smoke from recent days. In Beau's cruiser, remnants of the scent lingered and he immediately lowered all the windows as they began to move through the quiet streets. At the first stoplight he turned and reached to the floor behind Sam's seat.

"Here. Something for you," he said, lifting her jewelry box and setting it in her lap.

Sam hugged the box to her chest, immediately feeling its calming effects and absorbing the warmth it transmitted into her arms. Her mood dipped, however, as she thought of Sarah Williams and the funeral tomorrow.

Chapter 20

Sam coaxed Nellie and Ranger into the backseat of her pickup truck. The dogs seemed a little unsure of the surroundings—the parking lot of a convenience store where Sam and Kelly had agreed to meet before Kelly headed to Puppy Chic for the day—but they were typical canines, up for whatever adventure the moment presented. Beau had driven to another ranch a few miles away where he'd left the horses overnight. At last, their little family unit would be back home.

By the time Sam pulled through the stone gateway and down the long drive to the log house, Beau was leading Old Boy out of the horse trailer and through the gate into open pasture.

"Everything go okay?" Sam asked as she walked over to him.

"Just fine once they got over the idea that it might have been a trip to the vet."

She laughed. "I think the dogs felt the same way. Notice how they're hanging close to the front door."

"If you don't need to get to the bakery early, could you go through those documents with me? The ones you brought home last night. I'm having Kaycee Archer and Harvey Byron transferred to my office later this morning for questioning. It's a little complicated since the murder happened in the county, but they were arrested by the town PD."

"How about if I add a pancake breakfast to the deal?"

"Give me thirty minutes. I want to ride the fence line and make sure nothing along the east boundary was breached in all the hoopla yesterday."

By the time he came inside, Sam had two plates of hotcakes warming in the oven plus a bowl of fresh fruit and two flavors of syrup at the ready. While Beau washed his hands at the kitchen sink and assured her the property seemed relatively unscathed, she set everything on the table.

"So, what I found out is that there were about a hundred billion reasons someone would want Carinda Carter dead," she said once they doused their pancakes with syrup and began eating. "I didn't get far enough into reading the will, before they walked in on me, to know what Kaycee Archer's position is among all those half-siblings and cousins, but she seemed to think she would end up with a share that would provide Harvey Byron with the money he needs to get himself out of debt and to start a nationwide chain of ice cream shops. He made no secret that it had been his lifelong dream. I'm still not sure when he and Kaycee hooked up, although it does sort of explain her hanging around the fringes of the festival and his long absences from his booth."

"Did either of them admit to being the one who used the knife against Carinda?"

"No. In fact, they kind of started a blame game. It wouldn't surprise me if, under questioning, they end up turning against each other. I mean, having a lot of cash is one thing, being convicted of murder is something else. I don't see Harvey hanging around for that."

Beau chewed thoughtfully.

"I just got this feeling around Kaycee," Sam said. "She's not going to admit anything and she'll get herself the best criminal defense attorney money can buy."

"Do you want to be there when I question them?" he asked.

Sam thought of the mountain of work awaiting her at the bakery—the backdrops and displays from her booth that needed to be cleaned and put into storage, the phone calls to organize a meeting of the committee, and the business-as-usual amount of work at Sweet's Sweets as they ran headlong into the wedding season. Plus, it would probably be more interesting to see what story the two suspects gave Beau if they didn't know she had already briefed him on what to expect.

They cleared the dishes and neatened the kitchen together, then parted in the driveway.

"Remember, Sarah Williams's funeral is at two o'clock today," she said. "Join me if you can." She held up the hanger with the dressier clothing she'd decided to take into town with her.

He didn't sound too optimistic about his chances of breaking away. If he did put together enough evidence to arrest Kaycee or Harvey—or get lucky enough to extract a confession—his day would become filled with paperwork and formal procedures.

By 1:45, Sam was more than ready to get out of the bakery for awhile. True to her prediction, it seemed every bride in town had realized that June was here and they'd better get their cakes ordered. She had been training Jen to take orders for specialty cakes, but there was still a lot her assistant didn't know so Sam had been continually called away from the kitchen to answer questions or give ideas. More than one of the brides had been at the chocolate festival and demand was high for designs similar to Danielle Ferguson's winner.

At five minutes to two, she escaped out the back door, fanning the flush from her face as she started her van and headed toward the mortuary. Parking was nonexistent, the dash of more than a block left her face red and sweaty again, and the dolorous organ music automatically set off a rush of emotions as Sam found a seat near the back of the small room.

In the front row sat a few people who could be Sarah's relatives, although Sam didn't immediately spot Marc Williams among them. Odd. The next four rows contained an assortment of people, mostly older, mostly the simple country type who had probably consulted Sarah—and perhaps Bertha Martinez—for cures. A minister stepped forward when the music stopped, and it occurred to Sam that she had never heard Sarah mention a religious affiliation. Not that it really mattered now.

Words. Emotions. Memories. Wishes that she'd had more time with her friend. Tears dripped from her chin and Sam grappled in a pocket for a tissue. Questions in her mind about whether she could have learned more about Bertha Martinez or the history of the wooden box if Sarah had only lived longer. Perhaps the pace of the festival and her committee work had proved to be too much, and Sam wished she could rewrite the last few weeks to make better use of the time. Regret washed over her. But then, she supposed everyone must feel that way about someone who had died. We seldom leave every question answered or every situation resolved.

Thinking of unresolved situations took her mind back to the reasons Carinda Carter had died. At least Sam's relationship with Sarah had ended on a friendly note. Carinda's distant relatives were likely to be battling out their little war for years to come.

People began to stand and Sam realized the service must be over. She hung back, having little desire to stand in a line of strangers and shake hands with a lot of other strangers. Sarah was the only person in this room that she knew. She started to duck quietly out the rear door when she became aware of someone standing at her side.

"Are you Samantha Sweet?" a female voice asked.

Sam turned and nodded, taking in a woman of about forty, a bit taller than herself, with dark hair to her shoulders and honest green eyes. She wore black jeans and boots, a silky shirt in vivid jewel tones and a black hip-length jacket that looked expensive.

"You look just the way Sarah described you." The woman held out her hand. "I'm Isobel St. Clair."

Sam's expression must have given away her complete lack of recognition.

"I'm a historian, with The Vongraf Foundation." She studied Sam for a half-second. "We study historical artifacts, particularly items that have—shall we say—an element of the unexplained."

Sam felt herself backing away. Bobul's warning came back, about people who would take an interest in the carved box, people who would want to take it from her and use it for their own purposes.

"Are you certain that Sarah never mentioned me? She said she would get word to you."

Had she? Sam vaguely remembered Marc Williams mentioning someone when he told her of Sarah's final lucid minutes, back in the midst of the festival when Sam's mind hadn't focused on anything for more than a few seconds.

"Sarah's last days were—"

"I need to talk with you, Ms. Sweet, maybe now? Over coffee?" Isobel St. Clair chewed at her lower lip for a second, then she leaned close and whispered. "Lightning strikes once, makes three."

Bobul's words. Sam felt the blood drain from her face.

Chapter 21

Sam's hands shook as she inserted her key into the van's ignition. Now that it seemed she was on the brink of learning something about the wooden box she felt inexplicably terrified. She watched Isobel St. Clair pull out of the mortuary parking lot in a nondescript grey sedan that was undoubtedly a rental, heading the right direction for Java Joe's Joint where Sam had agreed to sit long enough for a coffee together.

Before putting the van in gear she dialed Beau's cell number.

"Hey, darlin'. Sorry I didn't make it to the service. But I've got good news—the Flower People cleared out. Middle of the night. I guess that's a good-news, bad-news situation. They didn't pay their fines and they left Mulvane's place a mess—"

"Sorry, honey, but I have an odd situation here. I'm about to have coffee with a woman and I'm not sure whether to trust her."

"Do you want me to come?"

"No." The sight of a uniform might undo everything Sam had hoped to learn. "But could you run a quick background check for me? See if a place called The Vongraf Foundation really exists. If so, does it look like legitimate historical research? And is there an Isobel St. Clair associated with it? If there's a chance to see a picture of her, is she about five-nine, in her forties, long dark hair and green eyes?"

"Okay . . . sure. Is there something I should know?"

"Just send me a quick text, let me know whether she's legit or not. I'll fill you in on the rest later." At the last second, she remembered to tell him where she was meeting the woman.

Isobel St. Clair was standing under the green awning in front of Java Joe's when Sam pulled into the tiny parking lot.

"Sorry, I had parked a block away from the funeral home," Sam explained.

Isobel regarded her with that direct gaze and suggested they might prefer an outdoor table at the far corner of the patio. They ordered at the indoor granite-topped counter and carried their beverages outside. The bistro-sized tables were wire mesh with matching chairs, not the most comfortable, but the attached umbrella kept the sun off. Sam selected the one chair with its back to the wall, wondering as she sat down if this would turn out to be another false or frustrating lead.

Isobel sat next to her, facing the back door of the

coffee house, watching the other two patrons as she reached into her small bag, brought out a leather case and pulled out a business card. Passing it to Sam she drew out a white envelope. Its battered corners and worn flap attested to the fact that the woman had carried it with her for some time. She handed it to Sam, as well.

The card had a logo—triangular, with a complex pattern that reminded Sam of Celtic knots—alongside The Vongraf Foundation. Isobel St. Clair's title was shown as Director. The telephone number was a Washington DC area code; address was a post office box in Alexandria, Virginia. Sam slipped the card into her pocket and placed her hand on the envelope.

Ms. St. Clair gave her a warning look as a young couple dressed in chinos and cotton sweaters came out to the patio. Sam vaguely recognized the girl as someone from Kelly's school days but neither of them gave her a second glance. She slid the envelope into her lap and lifted the flap. It contained a single photograph, very old by the look of it— of her wooden box.

"Ms. St. Clair, where did you get this?" Sam asked, leaving the picture in the envelope.

Her companion smiled. "You can call me Isobel. Let me give you a little history." She leaned back in her seat and began to speak softly.

"The Vongraf Foundation has been in existence almost since the founding of America. It is said that Benjamin Franklin, with his insatiable curiosity about everything— particularly about unexplained phenomena—was among the group of men who decided to take on the formal study of odd artifacts. Not that our research involves only physical items. Today, the foundation has branches that investigate everything from happenings in Egyptian tombs to celestial sightings over the plains of Peru."

"Sounds like the History Channel." Sam couldn't keep the note of skepticism out of her voice.

Isobel laughed. "I suppose it does. However, unlike television programs that tend to use words such as *could, would, might have* and *possibly* in their so-called fact finding, we deal in hard, verifiable facts. If an artifact comes to us, it is put through carbon-dating tests first, then it undergoes a battery of tests to ascertain whether any so-called 'magical' properties that its owners or local legend claim can be verified. The majority of the assertions involve contact with the afterlife or with extraterrestrials, along with a great number who say their item has healing properties or can cast 'spells' of some sort."

"And you have a huge warehouse somewhere in an underground bunker with all these mystical items stored in huge, dusty crates?"

"Hardly. Over ninety-five percent of the items we have ever examined prove to be either hoaxes or the test results are inconclusive. A small percentage actually do prove themselves to a degree, although oftentimes the evidence of healing or contact outside the earthly experience cannot be reliably duplicated. In other words, we see the unexplained action happen once or twice but it isn't as if the owner can replicate the action over and over."

Sam worked to keep her expression neutral. She had never experienced difficulty in getting the box in her possession to work its magic, any time she picked it up. She glanced again at the photo.

"And this?" she asked.

"There is more to this item than a simple case of 'does

it or doesn't it work'. We know for a fact that it does. The photo was taken during the foundation's testing of the item and documentation of its properties." She caught Sam's expression. "Way before my time, I will admit. Testing on this artifact was done in 1910. It was conclusively proven to be among the one-half of one percent—the items we see whose properties can be verified beyond a doubt."

"And now it's in one of those warehouses."

Isobel let out a little sigh. "You know it isn't. You know where it is."

Sam dropped the envelope on the table and started to rise.

"Wait! Sam, I don't want to take it. We have done our tests. We don't keep the artifacts; they stay with their owners. I was told you wanted to know about its history."

Sam's phone chimed with an incoming text message. She glanced at the readout quickly as she shuffled her pack and resettled in her seat. A single word from Beau— legit. She put the phone back, sent another fleeting look toward Isobel St. Clair. It was true. From the moment she had discovered that the wooden box gave her the power to heal, the power to see auras and fingerprints and things that others simply did not see, she had wanted—needed— answers. This might be her only chance to get them.

She nodded toward Isobel who had paused a moment to sip at her latte.

"Our archives show that the foundation has actually tested two boxes, nearly identical. Both showed remarkable power, in both cases we repeatedly duplicated the results." She set her cup down. "You know, I really should give you a bit more of the background."

Sam nodded.

"History suggests that at one time there were three boxes—hence the password I gave earlier, the mention of three . . ." She only mouthed the last word. "According to our tests, they were made from a single alder tree, a tree that had been struck by lightning. The molecular structure of the wood makes this point incontrovertible. The carving is not really *typical*, but I can say that it's in a *similar* style used by woodworkers in fifteenth century northern Europe, probably what today is Ireland."

Sam thought of her uncle who had lived in Galway and her pulse quickened a little.

"It would make sense, in those rather superstitious times, that a man who witnessed a lightning strike might believe the remaining wood to be . . . perhaps enchanted, or charmed in some way. He might gather the remains of the affected tree and take them home to make something from the wood."

From her own trip to Ireland, Sam could attest that the Irish were still a fairly superstitious lot.

"I mentioned that we found and tested two boxes."

Sam waited silently.

Isobel took a deep breath. "I don't like to use words like good and evil. They are subjective terms, and my background teaches me to deal in hard facts. Science. History. Things that can be documented."

She toyed with the plastic stirrer that came with the coffee.

"In this case, I think I can use those words. Partly based on historical data, partly on my own observations."

Evil? What was the woman talking about?

"I mentioned that your box was tested in 1910? Well,

the second one came to us in the 1970s. I'm still working on piecing together the history of it, but rumor says it may have been connected with Adolf Hitler." She held up a hand. "At this point, I cannot verify that and I hesitate to even mention it. It's just—"

Isobel stopped and took a long pull on her beverage, which had probably gone lukewarm by now.

"While the box was in our lab, one of the technicians had a very peculiar reaction to it. He was a man who tended to be a somewhat flamboyant personality anyway—artistic but driven— I don't know how to explain it, and I guess the reason Hitler's name came to me was that this technician's co-workers described him in similar terms. I don't know—I wasn't there, of course. But during the filming of our tests— films I have watched—this technician did become a little . . . I have to say *crazed* after he handled the box. Sorry, that's not a scientific term but that's the best way I can describe it. He walked around the lab with the box hugged to his chest and he began spouting all kinds of political-speak, things about how the power was in the wrong hands and if he were in charge of the country all those dissidents and protestors would be silenced."

She stopped and made a waving motion, as if scattering the thoughts to the wind.

"Well, you don't need all the details. Just suffice to say that it went a lot further than that, his hate-speech. Mainly, it was the look in his eye—that's where the word evil comes to mind."

"Did he keep the box?"

"Oh, no. The files show that it was locked away, out of his reach, and he was dismissed from the foundation. It is also carefully documented that no one else who came in contact with it had the same reaction."

"What ever happened to it?"

"After the testing was complete, it was returned to the family of the man who had submitted it, in Germany. This is where my interest as a historian comes in. I've made several trips there. The box was sold at an estate sale after the German man grew old and died. The person who bought it was named Terrance O'Shaughnessy."

Sam's uncle. She had already seen where the story was leading. When Uncle Terry died last fall, she had been given permission by his attorney to keep his box. She'd had it in her possession—that evil box—except that it had disappeared before she ever left Ireland.

"Do you know where it is now?" she asked.

Isobel shook her head. "I don't."

"And what about the third one? You said there were probably three?"

"The Vongraf's early research suggests that the third one was quite likely destroyed at some point in time. There are old books and diaries—witnesses who describe it being burned."

Bobul had once told Sam he'd witnessed the burning of a witch when he was a child in Romania, that the witch held a wooden box in her hands as she burned. He'd told Sam the box's magic powers had caused it to survive the fire.

"I'm making this my life's work, Sam. The historian in me is battling the scientist inside, well, at least wanting to break away and just do an old-fashioned hunt. A quest, I suppose you would say. I'm taking a leave of absence from my office duties at The Vongraf for awhile. I just want to see and verify the existence of each of the boxes. I don't want to take them away from their current owners; I don't want to own them myself. Just to see, to hold, to document."

The green eyes held Sam's for a long moment.

"I traced the one box—the one I'm calling the good one—as far as Bertha Martinez here in Taos. She received it as a child, from an uncle who fought in World War One. I knew she had passed it along to someone, not a relative, and when I found Sarah Williams . . . well, she told me that you had it. I'm asking you to trust me long enough to let me see and touch it."

"I'd like to think about it," Sam said. The more she was learning about the box, the more she realized that it could have a significance beyond anything she had ever imagined. She wanted to know more of the specifics of Beau's background investigation of Isobel St. Clair before agreeing to anything.

"That's wise," Isobel said. "I am not the only one with an interest."

She turned to stare at their surroundings. The other four people on the patio had left. Isobel sighed.

"There is a rival institution known as OSM. We think it might stand for something like Office for the Study of Mysticism, but no one says that. Their research goes more toward the occult and mystical than that of The Vongraf. Their science is faulty, but their interest is real. And potentially deadly. There are ties to high government officials—not only in this country, mind you—who want the power of these boxes out of private hands. It has happened in the past; during the Spanish Inquisition we believe one box was taken from its owner and stored deep within the

Vatican for centuries. These days, who knows what would happen to them, particularly if these same officials should get hold of both the good box and the evil one. It's a vital reason why I want to study the power behind the boxes— to see if there is a way to test for the ramifications if the two boxes should ever come together. It's possible that the result could be cataclysmic."

Government powers? Good and evil? Sam struggled to get her mind around it.

"Use great caution, Sam. Seriously. I know that someone from the other facility has been here in Taos recently, digging for information. Marcus Fitch. He got very close to Sarah Williams by posing as her long-lost nephew."

"Marc Williams?" Sam's head spun with the news. "But he seemed so nice, so sincere."

"He would. He was an undercover agent before he left the CIA to join OSM. He can act out nearly any role. But his motives are frightening. Do not trust the man."

Sam thought of Sarah's early confusion when admitted to the hospital under the watchful eye of her 'nephew.' Had Sarah's illness and death been engineered by this man? Perhaps to draw Sam into admitting she owned the box?

"I hate to say this, but I'm beginning not to trust anyone." Sam picked up her pack and stood. "I want to check this out. I'll be in touch."

"Thank you. That's very wise of you." Isobel rose from her chair. "You have my card. I'm staying at the Taos Inn for two more days."

Sam followed the historian back through the coffee shop and watched her get into the grey rental car. In her van, she phoned Beau.

"Yeah, I'm on my way home now," he said. "Kaycee

Archer and Harvey Byron spent the afternoon squabbling and then she promptly lawyered up. He's swearing she planned everything. She says he provided the knife. In the midst of all the 'he-said, she-said' I gather that they confronted Carinda together in the garden and when Carinda laughed at Kaycee's demand for a share of the Joffrey estate Kaycee went berserk, snatched the knife and stabbed her. We know it was one blow, just unlucky for Carinda that it went straight into her heart. Harvey, away from Kaycee, admitted it shocked him so badly that he rushed inside and threw up before he could go back to his booth."

Amazing, Sam thought, that Harvey had managed to work at all, to keep up the pretense for two more days. The man clearly had a hard streak she'd never witnessed.

Beau continued, "Other than organizing all the evidence we gathered and handing it over to the DA, looks like I'm done with this case."

"Harvey Byron. I have to admit I never saw that coming," she said as she started her van. "I'm leaving Java Joe's now. Kind of eager to hear what else you learned about Isobel St. Clair when I get home."

He met her at the door with a kiss and they settled into chairs on their back deck, overlooking open fields and the pasture where the horses grazed contentedly. The recent fire had taken only their easternmost field with the corn crop but Sam still cringed at how easily it could have passed the barbed wire fence between there and the barn.

"So, The Vongraf Foundation does indeed do historical research," he said, popping the top on a beer can. He continued, verifying everything Isobel had told Sam. "She's been with the foundation for fifteen years, basically from the moment she graduated from the University of Virginia. Still lives within twenty miles of where she grew up, although she has traveled quite a bit in Europe and the Mediterranean countries, a few times to Mexico. Never married but there was a fiancé a few years back. I've got the report and her picture in the house."

Sam popped up to get the information. The photo was definitely the woman she'd spoken with and the story seemed to check out. She remembered Isobel's warnings about the rival institution.

"Can I ask another favor?" she said to Beau, putting a little flirtation in her voice.

"You know you can." One blue eye winked.

"A man named Marcus Fitch at a place called OSM, also located in the DC area. Isobel said it stands for Office for the Study of Mysticism but might have another, more government-sounding name.

He jotted a note and promised to find out what he could.

They watched the sunset, grilled some burgers and found themselves yawning in front of a TV comedy when they decided to go to bed early. Although Sam had nearly dozed on the sofa, once the light went out upstairs she found her mind zipping over the day's events and the new information about the box. She'd wondered about the odd artifact for nearly two years—now that she knew a bit of its history she wondered if she should fear for its safety. Or her own.

The hour on the clock turned to single digits before she drifted to sleep.

Chapter 22

Isobel St. Clair thanked Sam when she called the next day. She invited the researcher out to the ranch, purposely choosing a time when Beau planned to be working on the property. Isobel showed up in jeans and a short-sleeved green cotton sweater that highlighted her eyes. She carried a bulky manila folder.

"I guess my résumé checked out," Isobel said with a tilt of her head toward the department cruiser parked beside the house.

"As you cautioned me yesterday, a person can't be too careful." Sam showed her into the sunny living room and offered tea, which Isobel declined, before bringing the wooden box out of the china hutch where she had temporarily stashed it.

"Ooh. I've read so much about this. It's amazing to be

able to touch it." Isobel set her folder on the dining table and took the box from Sam, handling it with a gentle touch. "I'd like to compare it to the notes—"

"Certainly. I would be interested in seeing them."

Isobel opened the lid. "The hinges were replaced at some point. These are not original. But look at the faint markings along the inside of the lid. They are unreadable now but we can see that they were here. According to the records, the other boxes also had words inscribed in this location. The stones—most likely they weren't put here by the carver; people in those times tended to have specialized trades and a woodworker probably didn't have the tools or expertise to grind, polish and mount these. But they are of the same period. Perhaps he took the box to someone else for the ornamentation."

She looked up. "It's definitely the same one The Vongraf studied, over a hundred years ago."

"The other box—the one in Ireland—" Sam hesitated for a moment. "It also had stones."

"Ah, I thought you may have seen it," Isobel said. "I had already discovered that Mr. O'Shaughnessy was your uncle."

Sam almost laughed. "You probably knew that before I did. A year ago, I had never heard of him. But he was a kind man. Beau and I went to Galway on our honeymoon and I was able to visit Terry's home."

"And to see the other box?"

"Actually, I handled it a little."

"But the box isn't still in your uncle's home. I was contacted by the estate attorney because he left some papers to the foundation. I asked about the box."

"Uncle Terry gave it to me. It disappeared from the

back seat of our car there in Galway. I would swear there was no one around when it happened, and Beau and I were never very far from the car. I have no idea who took it. I almost believed the box had somehow vanished under its own power."

Isobel didn't laugh or denigrate the idea. She merely stared down at the box in her hands now. Sam watched the way Isobel touched the box with reverence before handing it back. The box was cool to the touch when Sam took it. She had learned a lot about this thing, but to know more she knew she needed to trust someone. This was probably the person.

"Isobel? You're right about the boxes. They do have some type of magic, and it only works with certain people. Bertha Martinez told me I was meant to have this one, but it was long after her death that I figured out what she meant." Sam held the box between her hands, in front, where Isobel could see. "Watch what happens."

The dull wood began to warm and brighten, becoming a soft golden brown as Sam held it.

"Touch."

Isobel reached out and laid her palm against the top, pulling it back quickly. "It's hot!"

"Not yet. But it will get that way."

The smooth stones began to glow red, green and blue—brighter and brighter.

"How—?" Isobel backed slightly away, her eyes wide.

"Don't worry. This is the good one, remember? I don't feel like I have an evil gleam in my eye or anything." Sam set the box on the table. "Usually, once I've done this, I seem to have some degree of healing ability. I think it's the same thing that made Bertha Martinez such a renowned healer in her day. Sarah Williams confirmed that she'd seen Bertha do some pretty unexplainable things."

Isobel seemed fascinated. "I woke up this morning with a crick in my neck—hotel pillow. Do you think—?"

Sam stepped toward her. "Let me touch the spot." She held both hands gently against the sides of the younger woman's neck.

"Warm! I can't believe it." Isobel stood perfectly still. When Sam removed her hands, Isobel turned her head side to side. "There is absolutely no pain! I could hardly look over my left shoulder this morning."

She reached up and touched her neck in amazement.

"I'm not a healer," Sam said, "I'm a baker. I have no idea how this thing works or why Bertha wanted me to have it."

Isobel fixed a serious stare on her. "Take great care, Sam. I am still learning about these things, but from what I gather these boxes come into the possession of the right person at the right time. There is a reason you are supposed to have this one. Be careful that the wrong people do not get it."

Sam felt the weight of her mission.

"But the other one? If it's supposedly evil, why did my uncle have it? He seemed to be a gentle and happy man. I never heard that he did anything bad. He was certainly kind and generous with those who knew him."

Isobel chewed at her lower lip for a moment. "We don't know that yet, do we? Perhaps the third box still exists and it's the one he owned. Or maybe, as we've discovered just now—your box worked no magic when I touched it— maybe the evil box has no effect unless an otherwise evil person gets it."

She laid a hand on Sam's forearm. "Just be careful. I can't warn you enough. Don't ever forget that there are others who would love to get hold of this."

"The institute known as OSM?"

"And perhaps others. I need to go now," Isobel said, picking up her file. "Keep that artifact in a safe place. One day, the answer will come to you—the name of the person who is meant to own it next."

Sam watched the grey sedan drive toward the road, feeling a little shaky inside with this new knowledge. It seemed the box's days of sitting on her vanity in the bathroom, filled with costume jewelry, were over. She shoved aside the coats in the hall closet, opened the wooden panel at the back, and twirled the dial on Beau's safe. The box seemed a little forlorn when she set it inside and closed the door.

"All's okay?" Beau asked when he came in ten minutes later. "The historical lady friendly enough?"

She filled him in, including the parts about the box in Ireland being made by the same carver, the age of the boxes, and the interest of The Vongraf Foundation. Omitted the parts about the battle of good and evil and the fact that the box they had left behind in Ireland could very well be one of the latter. Those were the sorts of things Beau saw more as movie elements than reality, and for all Sam knew, that was exactly what they were.

His phone rang as Sam was heading toward the kitchen with a loose plan to figure out what to make for lunch. When his voice went still and then he said *uh-oh*, she turned. He clicked off the call and headed for the front door.

"Your friend—Isobel—she was involved in an accident. Just now, between here and town."

"I'm coming with you." Sam grabbed her pack and

trailed about two inches behind him.

His cruiser's wheels spun a little on gravel when he put it in gear. Lights on and siren wailing—they came to the accident scene less than five minutes later.

Isobel's grey rental sat nose down in a ditch beside the road, the driver's side door bashed. Sam felt her breath catch. Another Sheriff's Department cruiser was already on scene and a deputy Sam didn't know greeted Beau. She flung herself out of his vehicle and raced to the wrecked car.

The historian hung awkwardly by her seatbelt, blood running down the side of her face and a nasty gash on her left arm.

"Isobel! Isobel!" Sam shouted through the passenger side window, which had broken into a million tiny pieces.

"I'm okay," Isobel said, fumbling one-handed at the release button for the seat belt. "I just need to get this—"

"Don't! You're at such a weird angle—you'll fall. EMTs will be here in a minute."

"It was Marcus Fitch," Isobel said. "He came out of nowhere, behind me. He pulled alongside and I thought he would crash head-on with this other car . . . but he steered right into me. Pushed me off the road."

Her face suddenly went very white and her eyes rolled back as she slumped limply against the safety restraint.

Sam looked for Beau, who was talking to a man, apparently a witness, driving an older SUV. She started to run toward him but nearby sirens told her the ambulance had arrived. She hung back while emergency personnel crawled into the car, maneuvered Isobel out of it, and strapped her to a gurney. She was conscious again by that time and Sam stepped to her side.

"He went through my car," Isobel said breathing heavily. "Looking for the box . . . demanding it . . . took my file . . . and the old photo—from my purse—" Paramedics had laid the purse on her belly and she patted it. "Watch out. Please be careful."

One of the paramedics asked Sam to step out of the way and she watched helplessly as they loaded the woman into the ambulance.

"Her injuries seem pretty minor," he told Sam. "She'll be in the ER for a little while but they'll probably let her go home later today."

Not to Virginia, Sam thought.

Beau had finished questioning the witness and he walked over to Sam just as the ambulance pulled away. "The guy got a plate number," he said.

"I can do better than that. I got a name."

She went into the short version of how Isobel knew Marcus Fitch, that he worked for the OSM, saying only that there was an intense rivalry between their employers over some artifacts.

"I should go to the hospital to see how she's doing and to give her a ride back to her hotel when they let her out. She's all alone here."

She thought of the wooden box all the way home and throughout her drive to the hospital. How much harm was the thing worth? She would be better off to get rid of it, but she had tried that in the past and every plan backfired. Bobul's words came back to her, the things he had told her more than a year ago when he first showed up at her shop to make chocolates for the Christmas season. The boxes had a long history and they held immense power.

Good power and evil power. Sam had been entrusted with one of them, but it was not her job to right all the world's wrongs or to step into the midst of a battle between two competing organizations.

She rounded a curve in the road and pulled into the nearest parking spot to the emergency entrance. Inside the ER, she followed the sound of voices until she found Isobel St. Clair sitting on the edge of a bed, two butterfly plasters across the cut on her temple and a stretch of gauze encircling her arm.

"She'll have some facial bruising," said the nurse, "but all in all, she cleaned up pretty well."

She turned back to the patient and gave some instructions regarding the bottle of pain meds she was handing over, as well as some basic wound-care information.

"That was a little bit close," Isobel said as Sam helped her into the bakery van. "I really didn't think Marcus Fitch and the OSM were quite that desperate."

Sam got into her own seat and started the engine. "Well, you used the word 'evil' before. This looks pretty mild for true evil."

"I suppose you're right. At this point, all he wanted from me was to know what I knew. Guess he thought that since he couldn't butter me up with niceties and lunches, back in DC, that he would put a little scare into me. Don't worry, Sam, I did not and will not ever let them know that I've seen one of the boxes or where it is."

Sam thought again of the term 'evil.' Marcus wasn't going to stop at questioning. Eventually, this would lead to greater injuries, perhaps even torture, to get the information.

"He got my file," Isobel said. "For now, that should keep him happy."

"But all your work—lost."

"Everything I brought on the trip was a copy. The Foundation has excellent security on the premises and we're very careful about what actually gets out the door. I will be back behind those closely guarded doors by this time tomorrow," she said as Sam pulled up in front of Isobel's hotel room.

Sam didn't feel nearly as confident as Isobel sounded, but she was happy to drop her off with the assurance that she would immediately request a move to a different room for the night.

"He may figure out that I visited you, might have been watching while we talked yesterday. But nothing in that file leads to you. I was in town to see Sarah Williams, as he was, and that's the only connection he has to you. Stick with your story that you and Sarah had nothing in common but the chocolate festival."

Sam drove away, feeling a little queasy inside. At one point she had wondered if Marcus, posing as Marc Williams, might have killed Sarah. That probably wasn't the case—he had nothing to gain by Sarah's death without first getting his hands on the box. But the frightening thought that she had not voiced to Isobel was, had Marcus come a lot closer than any of them realized? Was he the man Rico had chased away from their home as the fire was moving in? If he'd not been caught, would he have broken in and ransacked their place in the same way he'd gone through Sarah's?

She quelled that thought. The box was well hidden. The dogs would not be away from the house next time and would defend the place with all their might. And, since causing Isobel's accident, surely the man knew enough to get away and stay away from Taos.

Chapter 23

Sam fell onto the sofa the moment she got home. When Beau walked in she peered out from under the arm she'd slung across her eyes to block the light.

"Busy week, huh?" he said, kneeling beside her to plant a kiss on the tip of her nose.

"Two mysteries solved in as many days," she said. "I learned what I wanted to know about Bertha's wooden box, you caught a murderer."

"I hope so." He sat near her feet. "I fully believe that Kaycee actually stabbed Carinda Carter, but I'm still not convinced that Kaycee and Harvey won't muddle each other's stories to the point where neither of them goes to prison."

"It was really luck of the draw that Carinda inherited the Julia Joffrey money in the first place, wasn't it? I mean, old Julia could have randomly chosen any of her many half-nieces or nephews. Maybe all she really wanted to accomplish was to throw the entire clan into a battle."

"Proof positive that winning isn't always a good thing, or a guarantee of happiness. I think you said that to me recently."

He smiled and stroked her leg. "Oh, I meant to tell you . . . I did what I could to get information on that OSM organization you asked about? Came up with zilch. It's as if they don't even exist."

Isobel had told Sam the group was pretty low-key, perhaps even a secret branch of the government. Maybe it was true.

"I can keep checking," he said. "I've got a couple of buddies in the FBI."

"Nah, that's okay." What good would the information do? It wasn't as if Sam planned to take them on, to track down Marcus Fitch—for what?—to pin a traffic accident on him? Let that battle remain Isobel's quest. She would keep the box locked away until she could decide what to do—keep it, figure out a way to destroy it, or—better—pass it along to its next rightful owner.

Meanwhile, the chocolate festival was finished and Sweet's Sweets would return to the normal, crazy pace of the wedding season. The Joffrey fortune would most likely end up being redistributed to dozens of beneficiaries and, with luck, at least some of them would put the money to use for some greater good. Life, for Sam and Beau, would settle— she hoped—into a state of contented bliss, unmarred by the high dramatics that Isobel St. Clair and her foundation found so intriguing.

She sat up and reached out to her husband, running an index finger along his jawline.

"Did I ever happen to mention how happy I am that you're my partner in this life?"

His deep blue eyes sparkled. "You might have, once or twice."

Author Notes

This story was great fun because, after all, what could be better than creating an entire festival that's all about chocolate! As much as I would love to take full credit for coming up with all the fabulous cakes and desserts portrayed here, I must admit to taking inspiration from many sources. The five finalist cakes in the competition, in particular, were based on photos I spotted in the lively baking community on Pinterest. Readers can go to my Pinterest board titled Cakes That Have Inspired Me and see just what I was looking at as I described each of them.

For the latest news on Connie's books, announcements of new releases, and a chance to win great prizes, subscribe to her monthly email newsletter!
http://connieshelton.com

Follow Connie on Twitter, Pinterest, and at Connie Shelton Mystery Author on Facebook

Books by Connie Shelton

THE CHARLIE PARKER MYSTERY SERIES
Deadly Gamble
Vacations Can Be Murder
Partnerships Can Be Murder
Small Towns Can Be Murder
Memories Can Be Murder
Honeymoons Can Be Murder
Reunions Can Be Murder
Competition Can Be Murder
Balloons Can Be Murder
Obsessions Can Be Murder
Gossip Can Be Murder
Stardom Can Be Murder
Phantoms Can Be Murder
Buried Secrets Can Be Murder
Legends Can Be Murder

Holidays Can Be Murder - a Christmas novella

THE SAMANTHA SWEET SERIES
Sweet Masterpiece
Sweet's Sweets
Sweet Holidays
Sweet Hearts
Bitter Sweet
Sweets Galore
Sweets Begorra
Sweet Payback
Sweet Somethings
Sweets Forgotten
The Woodcarver's Secret

Connie Shelton is the author of two internationally bestselling mystery series. She has taught writing courses and workshops, and was a contributor to *Chicken Soup for the Writer's Soul*.
She and her husband currently live in New Mexico.